Captain Kate

More Historical Fiction by Carolyn Reeder

ACROSS THE LINES
BEFORE THE CREEKS RAN RED
FOSTER'S WAR
GRANDPA'S MOUNTAIN
MOONSHINER'S SON
SHADES OF GRAY
THE SECRET PROJECT NOTEBOOK

CAPTAIN
KATE

Carolyn Reeder

A Children's Literature Paperback

CHILDREN'S LITERATURE
7513 Shadywood Road
Bethesda, MD 20817-2065

Copyright © 1999 by Carolyn Reeder

Library of Congress Catalog Card Number 98-24845
ISBN 13: 978-1-890920-14-2
ISBN 10: 1-890920-14-2

www.childrenslit.com

Second Children's Literature Printing: June 2006
First Children's Literature Printing: November 2002
First Avon Camelot Paperback Printing: January 2000
First Avon Camelot Hardcover Printing: February 1999

Printed in the U.S.A.

10 9 8 7 6 5 4 3 2

Summary: Determined to take her father's coal-carrying barge on the C & O
Canal from Cumberland, Maryland, to Georgetown in D.C., 12-year-old Kate
learns hurtful truths about herself.

For Barb Smith,
who bicycled the towpath with me

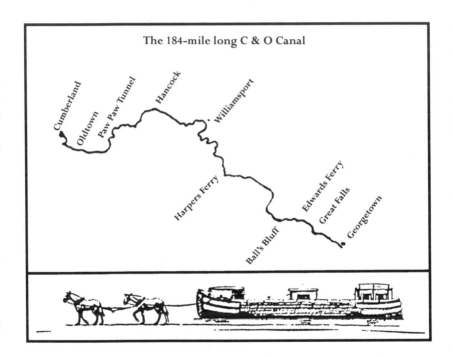

The 184-mile long C & O Canal

Cumberland
Oldtown
Paw Paw Tunnel
Hancock
Williamsport
Harpers Ferry
Ball's Bluff
Edwards Ferry
Great Falls
Georgetown

Captain Kate

Chapter One

Kate watched Seth run a few sideways steps before he let his first stone fly. Silently she counted the skips it made on the surface of the canal. Only three? She could do better than that with her eyes closed—she hadn't spent her whole life on the C & O Canal for nothing.

The canal *was* her whole life, Kate thought as she walked along the towpath beside her stepbrother while he skipped one stone after another. The canal, the boat, the mules that towed it, the—

"Hey, you'd better pull up your bonnet, Kate."

Startled out of her reverie, Kate frowned, and Seth said, "Don't you remember? Your mother told me to make sure you kept your bonnet on so you didn't get any more freckles."

Kate's hazel eyes flashed, but she kept her voice even. "She said to *remind* me to keep it on, and you've done that, but you can't *make* me do anything." The nerve of him!

1

Besides, the freckles across her nose were hardly notice-able—fairy's dust, Papa had called them. Kate swallowed hard. Even after almost a year and a half, the edges of the hollow place left by his death were still raw.

How could Mama have married again so soon, and married a singing teacher at that? And worst of all, how could she— Kate picked up a stone from the edge of the tow-path and threw it with all her might. It sailed diagonally across the canal and hit the railroad track with a resounding *clank*, just as if she'd planned it that way.

"I never knew you were such a tomboy," Seth said.

Hearing the disapproval in his voice, Kate bent to pick up another stone, a smoothly rounded one this time, and with an effortless flip of the wrist she sent it skimming across the water. "Six skips," she said smugly. Now he'd know just how much of a tomboy she was.

"Show-off," Seth muttered. He jammed his hands in his pockets and walked on.

Kate watched him with satisfaction. It was about time Seth found out that not all girls were quiet little ladies like his sister, Julia. Frowning now, Kate thought of how the younger girl was always helping Mama, always *with* Mama. At least Seth was usually out with his friends and not underfoot like nine-year-old Julia.

But after school today, Mama had asked Seth to go along when Kate went to check over the family's canal boat before this year's boating season began. Kate hadn't objected, because she knew her mother didn't think it proper for a "young lady" to walk alone through the busy industrial area that surrounded the boat basin. But she certainly didn't intend to "be nice to Seth," no matter how many times Mama told her to. Let Julia be nice, Kate thought. *She* was going to be in charge.

When the lumber mill and workshops along the north

side of the boat basin came in sight, Seth waited for Kate to catch up. "How do we tell your barge from all the others?" he asked, looking ahead at the boats tied up along the basin's length.

"It's not a 'barge,' it's a canal boat. The best-looking boat on the C & O." Barge, indeed, Kate thought, though she could see how someone who didn't know any better might call it that. But a barge wouldn't have a cabin for the boaters at one end, a stable for their mules at the other, and a hay house for the mules' feed in the middle. A barge wouldn't have a rudder, either, because you didn't steer a barge. And Kate was pretty sure barges weren't towed by mules walking along a path on shore.

"Hello, there, Katie! Who's your friend?" a woman called from the first boat they passed. Her hair was tied back, and she had a broom in her hand.

"Hi, Mrs. Ames! This is Seth Hillerman, and he's not my friend. He's my stepbrother."

The woman's eyes brightened. "So your mama married again! Well, I'm not surprised. Life's hard for a woman alone." She looked at Seth with interest. "And how old might you be, Seth?"

"Twelve."

"The same as Katie! Which of you is older?"

"I am," Seth said.

And Kate quickly added, "But our birthdays are only a week apart."

The woman smiled. "It will be nice for you to have someone your age along while you're going down the canal, won't it, Katie?"

"I'm taking Seth to see our boat now," Kate said, evading the question. She didn't want everyone on the waterway to know how she felt about her mother's marriage and the stepfamily that had been forced on her.

As they walked on, other boaters called out greetings, but Kate was eager to be on the boat again, so she just waved back and didn't stop to chat.

"There she is—*The Mary Ann*," Kate said at last, pointing to a white boat trimmed with red.

"You say this is the best-looking barge on the C & O Canal?" Seth sounded dubious.

"The best-looking *canal boat*. Come on." Kate nimbly climbed the wooden ladder Papa had nailed to the side of the boat. "I'll open the windows in the cabin to air it out, and then I'll show you everything," she said as Seth scrambled aboard. It was hard to stay out of sorts on *The Mary Ann*.

Eagerly, Kate led her stepbrother to the cabin and glanced around inside to see that everything was as it should be. Pots and pans hung from nails driven into the wall behind the small coal-burning stove in one corner. Dishes and the oil lamp were in place on the wide shelf along the wall, and some odds and ends of Mama's were on the small upper shelf next to Papa's cribbage game.

Kate let her eyes linger on the game for a moment before she turned her attention first to the row of oilskin raincoats that hung on pegs below the shelves, then to the wooden chairs arranged around the small table. The only other furniture was a rocking chair and the bedstead that stood against the opposite wall, ready for a fresh straw-filled mattress and the blankets they would bring from home.

"Isn't it going to be pretty crowded in here?" Seth asked as Kate chocked the window open. "This place can't be more than twelve feet on a side."

"It's not crowded, it's cozy," Kate objected.

"What about those other cabins?" Seth persisted.

"Those 'other cabins' are the hay house and the stable,"

Kate told him. "You'll sleep in the hay house like our hired hands always did."

As she led Seth up the few steps from the cabin, Kate pointed to a wooden lever in the stern. "That's the tiller—it steers the boat. We put up a canvas awning to shade the cabin and the captain." Gesturing, she explained, "The hold where they load our cargo of coal is under those hatch covers up there, and this is the race plank. It goes all the way around the boat." As she stepped onto the narrow ledge, she added, "I hope you have good balance, Seth, 'cause you have to walk on this to get by the cabin or the hay house and the—"

"Hey, be careful!" Seth cried.

Kate gave him a superior look and said, "*You* be careful. I've been doing this all my life. Come on, and I'll show you the hay house." She watched Seth ease his way along the race plank before she led the way to the small "cabin" in the middle of the boat.

"This will be filled with corn and hay for the mules, and you'll sleep there," she said, pointing to a shelflike bunk. "We'll have to pull out the trundle under the bed in the cabin for your sister." Kate thought of all the years she'd slept on that trundle, of how strange it had felt to sleep beside Mama in the big bed last year. Abruptly, she turned away from the hay house and said, "The stable's at the bow. That's the front of the boat," she added pointedly, leading the way.

"How do you get the mules off the boat?" Seth asked once he had stepped from the narrow race plank onto the hatch covers.

Showing him how a section of the stable roof lifted out, Kate said, "We use this for a ramp if we unload them at a lock." She waited for him to ask what a lock was, so she could explain how those narrow passages enclosed by solid wooden gates were used to raise or lower boats from one level of the canal to the next.

A lock is like a big step, Katie, Papa had explained when she was small. *Think of the river as a steep, rocky path going down a hill and the canal as stretches of smooth, flat walkways connected by steps.* Kate had looked across the towpath to the Potomac's rapids swirling alongside them and then back to the calm water of the canal, and she had understood at once.

Eager to explain how each lock was a giant step, Kate was disappointed when Seth simply peered into the stable and took a quick look at the harness and other equipment that hung from pegs in the wall. "What if you aren't at a lock?" he asked at last. "How do the mules get off then?"

"The same way you do, only they use that 'mule fall board,' " Kate said, pointing to a narrow platform that leaned ladderlike against the stable wall, "and we use this plank." She picked up a long board lying on the hatch covers and added, "We might as well put it in place right now, in case somebody wants to come aboard and visit."

"I'll carry that," Seth said, and he reached for the plank. But Kate ignored him and tucked one end of it under her arm. As she turned around, she felt the other end of the long board bump something, and she glanced back in time to see Seth slip off *The Mary Ann*, his arms flailing.

Kate dropped the board and ran to the edge of the boat just as Seth clawed his way to the surface of the water, gasping for breath. "I'll get a rope," she cried, but Seth was already struggling toward the ladder on that side of *The Mary Ann*, weighed down by his wool jacket and heavy shoes. Kate leaned over to help him, but he ignored her hand and pulled himself onto the boat.

"Don't you act so innocent," he said, teeth chattering.

Kate took a step back, speechless. He thought she'd pushed him in on purpose!

"Last week of March is a bit cold for swimming, laddie," a voice called from the next boat. "Better come aboard the *Captain's Fancy* and warm up at our stove."

"Thanks, Mr. O'Brian," Kate called, finding her voice. "Come on, Seth, you've got to get out of those wet things so you don't take a chill." She didn't want to have to put off the first trip down the waterway because her step-brother was sick.

Soon, Seth was wrapped in a blanket and sipping a cup of hot, heavily sweetened tea as they sat in the cabin of the neighbor's boat. "So how'd you manage to fall in, laddie?" Mrs. O'Brian asked as she hung Seth's clothes near the stove to dry.

"I didn't fall in. I was pushed."

"Oh, now, our Katie would never do a thing like that," the woman said, and her husband nodded his agreement.

Kate blushed. "I was carrying the plank, and I bumped him with it, but I didn't do it on purpose."

"Of course you didn't," Mrs. O'Brian said. Turning to Seth she asked, "What's your name, boy? I never seen you 'round here before."

"My name's Seth Hillerman, and I've never been around here before, ma'am. My father married Kate's mother last fall."

Mr. O'Brian raised his eyebrows. "So there'll be a new captain for *The Mary Ann* this year! What's your father's given name, Seth?"

But before he could answer, Kate quickly said, "Mama will be the captain, just like last season. Seth's father's gone off to fight in the war." How could the O'Brians think another man would ever take Papa's place at *The Mary Ann*'s tiller?

"Here, Katie," Mrs. O'Brian said, "have some of these cookies and then pass them to your brother."

Stepbrother, Kate corrected silently, reaching for the plate.

Chapter Two

It was early evening by the time Kate and Seth left the boat basin, and they walked without speaking until they were nearly home. "I didn't knock you into the canal on purpose, and you know it," Kate said at last.

"You did knock me in, though. I didn't just fall in, and I don't want anyone to think I did."

"Well, you'd better not tell people I pushed you," Kate retorted. "You know very well it was an accident."

"You'd better make sure there aren't any other accidents, or— Say, there's a buggy parked in front of the house."

"That's Dr. Smith's buggy!" Kate exclaimed, and she began to run. As she burst through the gate, she saw Julia huddled forlornly on the front porch, her face as pale as her corn-silk colored hair. Something must have happened to Mama! "What's wrong?" Kate demanded, stopping in front of the younger girl.

"I—I don't know," Julia said, shrinking away. "She—"

But Kate's attention had turned to the doctor, who was letting himself out of the house. "Is Mama all right?" She had to be all right, or Dr. Smith wouldn't be leaving, would he?

"There, now, Katie. She's going to be fine, but she needs to stay off her feet for a while. Mrs. Steller from next door said she'd be glad to help out, and I'm sure you children will be a big help, too. Isn't that right?"

Seth and Julia nodded, and Kate said, "You'll be surprised how much we can do, Doctor." Turning to the others, she announced, "We'll start by scrubbing *The Mary Ann*'s cabin and making up the beds so we'll be ready to set off for Georgetown with our first load of coal on Saturday."

The doctor shook his head. "I'm afraid this is going to change your plans, Katie. Your mama needs to rest in bed until after the—" He hesitated a moment and then said, "—Until the end of August, at least. Now be a good girl, and don't worry her."

Kate stared after Dr. Smith as he hurried along the walk to the gate. The end of August, she thought, a sinking feeling in her stomach. Boating season would be more than half over by then! The significance of that fact slowly dawned on Kate, and her almost overwhelming disappointment was quickly replaced by dismay. "How will we ever manage?" she whispered.

"I can keep the house neat if you fix the meals," Julia ventured.

"That's not what I meant at all," Kate cried. "What are we going to do for *money*? Money for rent, and for food and shoes for all of us next winter? Money to pay off our debts? Mama was counting on a good boating season to make up for the last two years, when the canal was closed so much because of the war."

Kate shuddered, trying to forget that battles had been

fought almost within sight of the towpath and that artillery shells had been fired back and forth across the Potomac more than once. Then, remembering how the enemy had damaged the canal and its locks and destroyed canal boats the previous autumn, she said grimly, "I hate those Rebels."

"So do I," Julia agreed. "If it weren't for them, there wouldn't be a war, and Papa wouldn't have had to go away to fight in it."

"He didn't have to go. He volunteered," Kate said.

"He volunteered to get the hundred-dollar enlistment bounty," Seth retorted. "What do you think we've been living on since he left?"

Kate hadn't known about the bounty. "I still think he wanted to be in the army. I think he married Mama so he'd have somebody to look after you and Julia while he was gone."

Julia's eyes filled with tears, but Seth said, "It's more likely your mother married him so she'd have somebody to look after her. Even that woman on the barge thought so—you heard her say life was difficult for a woman alone."

"Mama's still alone, isn't she? And I don't see that her life's any easier, with two extra children and a baby on the way." When she heard Julia catch her breath and saw the surprise on Seth's face, Kate paused uncertainly—she hadn't meant to say anything about the baby. "We aren't supposed to know, but I heard Mama telling Mrs. Steller," she said, remembering the shock she'd felt when she overheard the "wonderful secret" Mama had shared with their elderly neighbor. Why did grown-ups want to keep everything about babies a secret, anyway?

"Besides," Kate said, turning her attention to Seth again, "I don't see that your father's doing much to 'look after' Mama, between not being here and not sending any money home, either."

"That's not fair! You know as well as I do that—" Seth stopped when the front door opened again and Mrs. Steller came out onto the porch.

The old woman's face lit up with a smile when she saw Kate. "Your mama was just asking if you and Seth were back, Katie. Why don't the two of you—and you, too, Julia—run up and see her while I go home and heat up something for your supper?"

"I'll go up by myself," Kate said quickly. "They can see her after I come downstairs."

"Well, maybe that would be best," Mrs. Steller said as she looked from Julia's tear-stained face to Seth's fisted hands. "Maybe that would be best," she repeated. "Go on up, Katie, but don't stay too long."

As Kate crossed the porch she heard Seth say, "Don't cry, Julia. As soon as the government pays the soldiers their back wages, Papa will send money home. We'll manage."

"But what if Mother—Kate's mother—dies? What would become of us?"

Kate stopped short, her hand on the door latch and her heart pounding so loudly she could barely hear Seth's reply.

"She's not going to die, Julia. You heard the doctor say that she'll be fine. She just needs to rest." He turned to Kate and demanded, "Well, are you going up to see her, or are you just going to stand there?"

Without answering, Kate went inside. Please be all right, Mama, she begged silently as she ran upstairs. Please, please, *please* be all right. She hesitated in the doorway of her mother's room. Mama's eyes were closed, and her dark hair was loose on the pillow. Kate had never seen Mama in bed in the daytime before, and she felt ill at ease, almost as though she were looking at a stranger.

A stranger. Sometimes *she* felt like a stranger in her own home, watching while Mama treated the *real* strangers like family. Her feelings a confused mixture of longing and anger, Kate backed away from the door and tiptoed to the stairs. When she reached the bottom step, where Seth and Julia were waiting, she said coldly, "You two can go on up now."

Kate watched them hurry up the narrow stairs and disappear down the hall toward Mama's room. She waited, listening, and when she heard her mother's voice, full of the warmth that had always made her feel so loved and wanted, Kate's eyes swam with tears. *She* was the one who should be with Mama. *She* was the real child, and they were only stepchildren. What was the matter with her? Why hadn't she gone in and hugged Mama and told her how frightened she'd been when she saw Dr. Smith's buggy, how glad she was that Mama was going to be all right? *Why?*

Kate ran outside, instinctively heading toward the mule shed at the far end of the long, narrow backyard. "Oh, Papa," she whispered, weeping as she fumbled with the latch. "Why did you have to die and leave me?"

Inside the shed, Kate buried her face against Cupid's neck and sobbed. Gradually, the big mule's warmth and the familiar sound of the four stablemates munching their feed calmed Kate, and she felt her hurt and anger drain away, leaving only emptiness. How would she stand being here in Cumberland when the canal was open? It had been hard enough the past two seasons during the months the waterway was closed because of the war.

The cozy cabin on *The Mary Ann* was her real home, Kate thought. The other boaters were her real neighbors, and the whole canal was her neighborhood. The narrow, three-story yellow house at the end of the lane here in Cumberland was simply the place she spent the winters. The place she stayed while she waited for boating season to begin—or for the canal to reopen after the Rebels had been chased back to their own side of the river.

How could she possibly wait until the end of August to go down the waterway? *The end of August.* Mama had told Mrs. Steller the baby would come in late August. "That baby's spoiling things for me before it's even born," Kate said bitterly.

All winter long, she had looked forward to boating season, to being on *The Mary Ann* again, and now she was going to miss it because of the baby. She'd miss the leisurely trip as the mules towed the boat down the waterway, miss seeing the wheat fields and mills and small river towns slip slowly past. She'd miss seeing the greening woodlands and the Potomac River alongside—sometimes rushing, sometimes placid, but always drawing her eyes to its beauty as it flowed eastward toward Georgetown and beyond.

Kate knew every one of the 184 miles between Cumberland, Maryland, and Georgetown, in the District of Columbia—where the bloodroot bloomed first in the spring, where the best berry patches were, where to find the juiciest pawpaws in September and the sweetest persimmons when the weather turned cool.

She knew all the lock tenders, too, and knew which of their wives sold the best fresh-baked bread. She knew which locks were tricky to take the boat through and where along the waterway you had to hug the shore. Papa had taught her just about everything there was to know about boating.

Kate leaned against Cupid and closed her eyes, remembering the way Papa had let her pretend to steer the boat, her small hand under his large one on the tiller. How proud she'd been when he first let her steer alone, and how confident she'd felt with him there beside her, ready to help if she needed him.

And then the last year of his life he'd let her take the boat through the easier locks. "Next year, you'll be ready to take her through some of the crooked locks," he'd promised, speaking of the more difficult ones. But when the next year came, he was gone.

That year—last year—Kate and her mother had steered the boat while two hired boys took turns driving the mules along the towpath. It had been terrible at first, missing Papa, but Kate knew he would have been proud of "his girls" for staying on the canal and managing on their own.

They'd managed just fine, too, Kate thought. It wasn't their fault that boating season had been cut short because of the war. And they'd have been ready to start the new season together next week if only Mama hadn't met the handsome new singing teacher at church.

"I hate him," Kate whispered. "He ruined my life." She'd been glad when her stepfather went off to war, glad she wouldn't have to see him sitting at Papa's place at the table anymore. A wave of grief flowed over her as she thought again of the evening Mama had sat down to supper and said, "Now this is a real family—three fine children gathered around the table with their parents."

But the *real* family was Papa, Mama, and me, Kate thought miserably. She had belonged to that family, been the center of it, but she felt like an outsider in this new family that meant so much to her mother.

Drawing a shaky breath, Kate reached for the brush and began to groom the mules. The familiar, rhythmic motions calmed her, and by the time she heard Julia calling, Kate felt in control again.

Chapter Three

"Do you want to take a tray up to your mother?" Julia asked tentatively when Kate came inside. "I can do it, if you'd rather."

"I'll do it," Kate said. "You two go ahead and eat." She picked up the tray and headed for the stairs, thinking that she would sit with Mama while she ate, hoping that would make up for—

"There's my Katie!" Mama exclaimed as Kate reached the bedroom door. "I've been waiting for you to come and see me."

"You were asleep when I came up before," Kate said, "or maybe just resting with your eyes shut," she added when Mama frowned. "I've brought your supper."

"What a pretty tray!"

Kate noticed for the first time that it was set with Mama's good china and one of her best linen napkins—and that purple crocuses from the backyard floated in a tiny bowl. "Julia fixed it," she said reluctantly.

Mama's smile faded, and she said quietly, "I do wish you and Julia could be friends, Katie."

Friends! It was bad enough to have to share her room with Little Miss Perfect.

Mama asked gently, "Katie, don't you think it's about time for you to accept Seth and Julia—and my marriage?"

Kate pressed her fingernails into her palms and asked, "Could we please talk about something else?" She didn't want to spoil the only time she'd had alone with Mama since she could remember.

"Of course we can—we haven't had one of our good chats for a long time, and I've missed them." Mama set her teacup back in its saucer and prompted, "What's on your mind these days, Katie?"

The same thing that's been on my mind for months, Kate answered silently—how Seth and Julia and your marriage have ruined everything for me. And now on top of that, I'm going to miss more than half of boating season, and I've been counting the days ever since Christmas. That's what's on my mind. To her dismay, Kate felt her eyes fill with tears.

Mama rested her hand on Kate's arm, and her warm touch and the concern in her voice made Kate's throat ache. "There, now, Katie, everything will be all right."

For a moment, Kate wanted nothing more than to believe that and to kneel beside the bed and be comforted, but instead she pulled away. "If you don't mind, I'll go downstairs now," she said, trying to keep her voice steady. Things would never be all right unless Seth and Julia and their father—and the baby—suddenly disappeared.

"Let me give you this before you go," Mama said, picking up a folded paper from the table beside her. "Would you and Seth take this to the Canal Company office after school tomorrow?"

Kate nodded and took the paper. At the foot of the stairs, she unfolded it, and her heart began to race as she read. Mama was going to rent out *The Mary Ann*—and the mules! How could she even think of such a thing?

Remembering Cupid's warm comfort, Kate thought indignantly, Papa never would have rented out his mules, no matter what. And he wouldn't have let anyone who wasn't family captain his boat, either. How could Mama possibly say that everything was going to be all right?

And then Kate was rocked by a terrible realization: The rental would be for the entire boating season. She wouldn't have to wait till the end of August to go down the waterway, she'd have to wait another whole year! Without a second thought, Kate tore the paper into tiny pieces and dropped them in her pocket.

But halfway to the kitchen, Kate stopped short. Tomorrow night Mama would ask if they'd delivered the letter, and when she found out they hadn't, she would simply write another one to send with Seth. And Seth would do anything Mama asked him to, Kate thought as she continued down the hall. He wouldn't care whether strangers neglected the mules, whether strangers treated them cruelly. Kate was frowning when she came into the kitchen.

"She isn't worse, is she?" Julia asked, a catch in her voice.

Kate shook her head and went to fill her bowl from the pot of stew Mrs. Steller had brought over for their supper. "Listen, Seth," she said, sitting down at the table. "Tomorrow night when my mother asks if we delivered her letter to the Canal Company office, I want you to say we did."

"What letter? What's this all about?"

"It's too complicated to explain."

"You ask me to lie for you, but you don't want to bother to tell me why? Forget it."

Kate looked across the table and saw that Seth's jaw

was set in a stubborn line. "All right then, I'll tell you. I don't want Mama to find out that I tore up the letter she wrote arranging to rent out the boat and the mules."

Seth set down his spoon and said, "I don't understand you, Kate. An hour ago you were worrying about your mother's debts, and now you're throwing away the perfect opportunity for her to make some money."

Kate said flatly, "I don't want anybody else taking our boat down the canal." Taking Papa's boat.

"Well, I don't think you have much choice, Kate," Seth said. "*You* certainly can't take it."

Kate stared at Seth as his words sank in. "Wait a minute," she said slowly. "You've given me an idea." Maybe she *could* take it! And then the boat and the mules would be treated the way Papa would want them to be, she wouldn't have to wait a year to go down the waterway again, and she'd be earning the money Mama needed. Mama would see that her *real* daughter could be counted on for more than setting a pretty supper tray.

Her mind racing, Kate looked at Seth appraisingly and said, "If you weren't scared, the two of us could manage *The Mary Ann*."

"Scared! What's there to be scared of?"

He'd risen to her bait! "I thought maybe you were afraid of the mules. Or of falling off the boat again."

"Now, wait a minute—" Seth began.

And Julia cried, "That's not fair! Seth's not afraid of anything, and he didn't—"

"What about hard work?" Kate interrupted, raising her voice. "Are you afraid of that?" she challenged.

"I can certainly work as hard as you can," Seth said.

We'll see about that, Kate thought as she picked up her spoon and stirred her stew. She was much too excited to eat. She wasn't going to miss boating season after all!

Keeping her voice calm, Kate said, "Good. It's settled then. Julia, you can take care of my mother while we're gone, can't you?"

"Wait a minute," Seth interrupted. "This afternoon you said it took at least three people to run a canal boat."

"Lots of them have just two men on the crew." Well, a few of them did, anyway.

"Two *men*, Kate. Not a boy my age and a girl."

She knew he was right, but Seth's patronizing tone angered her, especially the way he'd said those last three words. "So it will take us longer," Kate argued. "We won't be able to make as many trips as a boat with a full crew, but we'll still earn a lot more than we'd collect if we rented *The Mary Ann*." And no one would have a chance to mistreat the mules.

"But is it safe?" Julia asked hesitantly.

Kate gave her a scornful look and said, "Of course it's safe." If it weren't, the government would close the waterway again. Besides, after all the damage Rebels had done to the canal last fall, there would probably be even more Union soldiers guarding the Potomac River fords and ferry crossings, and even more army camps near the waterway.

"It's settled, then," Kate repeated, careful not to let her excitement show in her voice. "Tomorrow morning Seth and I will go to the boat basin to buy supplies and get our load of coal, and then we'll be on our way." She knew it would be hard with just the two of them—and with Seth not knowing the first thing about boating—but they'd manage. And she could hardly wait!

"But will your mother let the two of you go all by yourselves?" Julia asked.

Her stepsister's question jolted Kate. "Mama won't know we're gone till it's too late to stop us," she said, planning as she spoke. "She'll think we went to school and then took her letter to the Canal Company office, and by the time she finds out we didn't, we'll be miles away." And once Mama was used to the idea, she would be grateful, Kate told herself as she began to spoon up her stew. Mama would be glad she didn't have to rent *The Mary Ann* and the mules, glad to be able to pay off her debts.

Julia stared across the table at Kate. "You mean you're going to leave without even telling her good-bye?"

"That shouldn't surprise you, Julia," Seth said, his voice hard. "You've seen how Kate treats her mother—barely speaking to her, never offering to help, acting like she doesn't love her at all."

Stung by his words Kate cried, "How dare you say a thing like that! Of course I love my mother—and I'm going to write her a good-bye letter, not that it's any business of yours." Pushing away the half-eaten stew, she left the table and stalked out of the kitchen, but in the hallway, she pressed herself against the wall and listened.

"How did she do that? How does she always manage to get her way?"

It was Seth's voice. Kate held her breath and waited for Julia's reply.

"She doesn't always. She couldn't stop her mother from marrying Papa, don't forget."

"Sometimes I wish she had."

Kate was shocked at the harshness of Seth's voice, and she waited to hear what Julia would say to that.

"But I like having a mother! And I like living in one place instead of traveling around while Papa gives singing lessons. Everything would be perfect if it weren't for Kate—and if Papa were here." Julia's voice was wistful.

Kate's mind reeled as she tiptoed down the hall to the stairs. Everything would be perfect if it weren't for Kate? She'd never thought about how Seth and Julia might feel about her—or about how pleased Julia would be to have Mama all to herself. Well, Kate decided, she didn't care one bit. She'd waited all winter for boating season to start again, and nobody—not Seth, not Julia, not even Mama—was going to cheat her out of it.

Papa would be proud of her, Kate thought as she climbed the stairs, proud of her for staying on the waterway and glad she wouldn't trust his boat and the mule teams to strangers. *We're a boating family, Katie,* he'd always said. *You'll not go wrong if you stay on the C & O Canal.*

Chapter Four

"Here, you can take Cupid and Junior, 'cause they're the gentlest," Kate said as she brought the first two mules out of the shed the next morning. "Go on, take hold of their leads—and be quiet."

Seth had made no secret of the fact that he thought mules were inferior to horses, and Kate watched him eye Cupid and Junior disdainfully as he took their leads. She went back into the shed for General and Sandy, remembering how Seth had assumed all mules were brown before he first saw Sandy's tan coat.

Kate had just strapped the flour sacks stuffed with sheets and blankets and extra clothing onto Sandy's back when Julia came running out. She wasn't going to try to stop them, was she?

"I packed you a lunch," Julia said, and she thrust a napkin-covered basket toward Kate.

Kate took it, realizing she should have thought of that

herself. Mama always packed a lunch for the first day. "Thanks," she said grudgingly. "And thanks for looking after my mother while I'm gone. Remember, don't give her the letter till suppertime."

"Are you sure you'll be all right, Julia?" Seth asked.

"Of course she will," Kate said before the younger girl could answer. "Besides, Mrs. Steller's right next door. Now come on." Kate led her mules out of the yard and waited for Seth to tell Julia good-bye and follow with his team. She grinned when he cringed and said, "Hey, you! Get your nose off me."

"That's why we call her Cupid," Kate said as Seth latched the back gate behind them. "She's very loving."

As she turned to start down the long, unpaved lane that led steeply toward the Potomac River and the canal alongside it, Kate heard Seth mutter, "Maybe you should take some lessons from her."

Kate stopped short and looked back at him. "Did you say something?" she challenged. If they were going to be together, day in, day out, all the way to Georgetown and back, he'd better know who was in charge. Seth shrank from Cupid's velvety nose again and didn't answer.

Satisfied, Kate turned away, but as she led General and Sandy down the hill, Seth's muttered comment began to needle her. He was wrong, Kate told herself. She *was* loving, or at least she used to be. She frowned when she remembered that her stepbrother had accused her of not loving Mama. Silently, Kate's lips formed the words, "But I do, and she knows I do."

Mama *did* know, didn't she? Of course she does, and if she's had any doubts lately, they'll be gone when she reads my letter, Kate told herself, thinking of the letter she'd poured her heart into after Julia had fallen asleep the night before. It was easier to put feelings into words on paper, easier to write the words than it was to say them.

Mama would understand, Kate reassured herself, and it didn't matter what Seth thought as long as he did his share of the work. Still, he had a lot of nerve to suggest that she should take lessons from a mule, even if the mule was Cupid.

As they neared the boat basin, Kate's spirits began to rise. This was what she'd been waiting for all winter—the start of boating season—and she wasn't going to let anything spoil it for her. Or anybody, either. It would be a good trip, Kate told herself. She knew exactly what to do, and the Rebels hadn't caused any trouble along the canal for months now, so there was nothing to worry about. *Except the tunnel.*

The familiar, almost suffocating fear threatened to sweep over Kate at the thought of the long, dark passage that took the canal and towpath through a mountain. To keep her mind off the tunnel, she concentrated on her mental list of the provisions they would need for the trip. They'd have to buy dried beans for soup, a wedge of cheese, lantern fuel. . . .

When they reached the towpath, a boat was approaching them, a young boy walking beside the mules. "That boat's a lot smaller than yours," Seth observed.

"All canal boats are the same size. Ninety-two feet long and fourteen feet wide." Kate saw Seth glance from the race plank to the water's surface, measuring the distance with his eyes.

"Well, this boat sure isn't anywhere as high as any of the ones we saw in the basin yesterday," he said.

"Those were 'light' boats—empty ones—and this boat's loaded with tons and tons of coal to take to Georgetown.

I'd of thought you could figure out for yourself that a loaded boat would ride lower in the water."

Seth's voice was tense, and his words left no doubt about how he felt. "Look, Kate, you don't have to act so superior. You may know everything there is to know about canal boating, but you don't know much else.

"Maybe you've been your hundred eighty-four miles down the canal and back year after year," he continued, "but I'll bet you've never been to New York or Philadelphia. Or even Baltimore. And you know what? Pretty soon, I'll have been to Georgetown—maybe even Washington City—and by then I'll know all about canal boating, too. And you won't know one thing more than you do today."

Kate felt her face grow warm. "Who's acting superior, now?" she asked.

"This isn't going to work, Kate. I think we'd better forget the whole thing."

He couldn't do this to her! "I might have guessed you'd be a quitter," Kate said, making her voice scornful. "Give me those mules."

Seth tightened his hold on his team's leads. "So now you think you can be a crew of one?"

"There's usually a couple of boys—or men—waiting to sign on to crew. I'll hire somebody."

"You can't do that!" Seth cried. "It wouldn't be—"

"Look," Kate interrupted, "you get this straight, once and for all. I'm taking *The Mary Ann* down this canal, no matter what. Are you coming with me or not?"

Seth glared at her and said, "I'm coming. Now move along."

Kate turned away to hide her relief that he hadn't called her bluff. Seth had more spirit than she'd thought, but he wasn't going to get the best of her.

Another loaded boat was approaching, and Kate forgot

about her stepbrother when she saw that it was *The Morning Star*, with Mrs. McLain, Mama's closest friend, at the tiller and her husband driving the mules. The family's oldest son shouted a greeting as he clumped across the hatch covers, and Mrs. McLain called for her husband to stop the team.

Kate's mouth went dry. "I just know she's going to ask where Mama is," she whispered.

But it was Mr. McLain who said, "Looks like you young-sters plan on taking *The Mary Ann* down the waterway all by yourselves, Katie."

For a terrible moment, Kate was sure her plan had been discovered, but then she saw the twinkle in the man's eye. She felt her pulse pounding in her temples, but she managed to smile and say lightly, "I guess it does look that way, Mr. McLain, but Mama's going to meet us after we buy our supplies and take on our load of coal."

"Is your Mama still feeling poorly, Katie?" Mrs. McLain called from the boat.

"She's doing better," Kate called back. "She's going to walk down to meet us later."

Mr. McLain said, "Well, hope you all have a good trip. Guess we'll be seein' you in Georgetown, if not before."

"Guess so," Kate said, waving good-bye. She wondered what the McLains would have thought if they'd known she and Seth really *were* taking the boat down the waterway by themselves.

"You're a pretty good liar, Kate. I'll have to remember that."

Turning on her stepbrother, Kate said, "Don't you dare call me a liar, Seth Hillerman! I'd never lie to keep from getting in trouble or even to get my own way, but this is different."

"Are you telling me this trip has nothing to do with getting your own way?" he asked, holding his ground.

"This trip has to do with making as much money as we can to pay off Mama's debts and save for next winter."

Seth gave her a scornful look and said, "You know very well that's not the only reason."

"You're right—it's not. The other reason is that I don't want to rent out Papa's boat and the mules." That was the most important reason, but deep down Kate knew that getting her own way had a lot to do with it, too.

"The boat basin is just ahead, and I still don't have any idea of what you expect me to do," Seth reminded her.

"First we tether the mules, and then you pole the boat to the wharf so we can get our supplies. After that, you pole us over to the coal company for our cargo and the waybill we turn in to get paid. When that's all done, I'll tell you all about driving the mules." And then we'll be on our way—provided nothing goes wrong.

Kate tried not to show her nervousness when they stopped first to have the hay house filled with feed for the mules and then to buy provisions at the general store. By the time the storekeeper added the last item—a box of cocoa—to the growing pile of goods on the counter, Kate could hardly wait for him to enter the cost of their purchases in his account book so they could leave. Her heart almost stood still when he looked over the top of his spectacles and asked, "Isn't your mama coming in to make sure you've remembered everything, Katie?"

Kate shook her head. "Mama's feeling poorly today, but we didn't want to wait any longer to start down the waterway." She picked up the can of lantern fuel and Seth slung the heavy cloth sack over his shoulder.

The storekeeper tucked his pencil behind his ear and asked, "You youngsters sure you don't want some help carrying all that?"

"Thanks anyway, Mr. Edwards, but we can manage," Kate said, certain that he didn't suspect a thing.

When they approached the coal dock a short time later, another boat was being loaded. It was positioned with its middle hatches under a coal car on the railroad trestle that spanned the boat basin. The car was heaped with coal, and at a signal, a trap door at the bottom opened and chunks of coal poured down a chute into the boat's hatches with a tremendous rumble. Kate hoped Seth noticed how the boat rode lower and lower in the water.

After *The Mary Ann*'s hatches had been filled, Seth poled the boat back to where they had left the mules, and Kate dipped up buckets of water to rinse off the worst of the coal dust. She could tell from the set of her stepbrother's mouth that he expected her to splash him, so she was especially careful not to.

When they were both on the towpath again, Kate said, "As soon as we put one pair of mules in the stable and hitch up the other pair to pull the boat, we'll be ready to start. I'll get the harnesses and the towline while you put the mule fall board in place so we can get General and Sandy on board. We switch teams every six hours," she explained. Ordinarily, they switched drivers every six hours, too, but Kate didn't want to think about that.

A few minutes later, Cupid and Junior were harnessed one behind the other, and the long towline was attached to the boat. Kate went aboard, and looking down at Seth she said, "Now, listen carefully so you'll know what to do. When you want the mules to go, you call 'COME up,'" she directed, dragging the first word out and dropping her voice on the second. "You keep saying it whenever they start to slow down."

"COME up," Seth repeated.

"And if I want you to stop the mules, I sing out 'Tee,

yip, YA-ah!' " The two notes of the YA-ah sounded almost like a little yelp.

"And how do I make them stop?"

"You say 'Whoa,' of course. Look, until we come to a lock, you just walk beside the mules and keep them moving. We won't come to the first lock for a long time, so I'll wait and tell you what to do then. And don't worry, it's easy enough."

At least it looked easy. Kate reassured herself that if last year's young drivers could do it, Seth could, too. She watched her stepbrother look dubiously from the long, narrow boat to the mules stomping impatiently in their harnesses. He wasn't going to back out now, was he?

"I'm ready when you are," Seth said.

"Let's go then," Kate said. Seth looked as though he didn't believe the mules would be able to pull such a load, but he kept his thoughts to himself and called for them to "come up." Kate watched Cupid and Junior walk effortlessly until the towline was stretched taut and the boat's dead weight brought them to a halt. She watched them lean forward and knew their eyes were bulging with the effort. They leaned and strained, leaned and strained, until at last they took a small step forward, and then they leaned again.

The mules continued this awkward cadence until the boat finally began to move. When Seth called for them to "come up" they flicked their ears and increased their pace. "So far, so good," Kate whispered. No one had even suspected what she—with Seth's unwilling help—was about to do. What she was doing!

Soon Kate began to relax, enjoying the feel of the boat responding to her firm pressure on the tiller. She saw that the mules were walking along briskly as Seth strode beside them, looking like he'd been a driver all his life. Except that he was wearing shoes.

"Tee, yip, YA-ah!" Kate sang out, wondering if Seth would remember that was the signal for him to stop the team. Almost instantly, the mules stopped, and Seth looked back at her. He learns fast, Kate thought as the boat drifted toward him. "I forgot to tell you to leave your shoes on board," she called.

"It's too cold to go barefoot," Seth called back.

Kate shrugged. "Well, it's your choice," she said, adding under her breath, "but I bet you'll wish you'd listened to me."

As she eased the boat a little to the right, she saw her stepbrother look across the canal and up the hill. She turned her eyes toward the hillside, too, searching for the house. There it was, with the sun reflecting from the up-stairs windows.

A wave of homesickness swept over Kate as she thought of Mama resting in her sunny bedroom. It didn't seem right to be here on the boat while Mama lay in bed at home, and Kate knew it wasn't right for her and Seth to be here on the boat while Mama thought they were at school with Julia.

Julia. Kate frowned as she remembered how pleased Mama had been with the supper tray Julia had fixed for her the night before. Mama liked that sort of thing. She was probably glad to have a stepdaughter like Julia, some-one sweet and ladylike, a pretty little girl who liked pretty things.

Kate sighed. She had no interest in being sweet and ladylike, and in spite of her hazel eyes and the thick, honey-colored hair that hung down her back, she had never thought of herself as pretty. As for pretty things, the ones she liked weren't the ones you could own or wear. They were things to appreciate and remember—bluebells blooming in the woods along the towpath as far as you could see . . . the whippoorwill's call on a summer night . . . an eagle soaring above the river . . . even the fierce beauty of lightning. Things she'd shared with Papa.

Papa. Kate swallowed hard. Sternly, she reminded herself that she'd felt sad at the beginning of the trip last year, too, missing him so much. But last year, Mama had been there to comfort her, and now—

If only Mama hadn't started going to singing classes at the church last spring during the months the canal was closed! Then she never would have met the handsome singing teacher with the pretty little daughter and the self-righteous son. Kate sighed, wishing she were starting down the waterway with Mama and a couple of boys hired to drive the mules instead of with Seth. Seth, who had never even been on a canal boat until yesterday. "Hey," she hollered, "can't you make those mules move faster?"

Her words seemed to startle Seth out of a daydream, and he stepped up his pace. He actually looked like he was enjoying himself, Kate thought in surprise. Well, walking in the late March sunshine with the river flowing past on your right and the calm water of the canal on your left was a nice way to spend the day. A lot better than sitting in a stuffy classroom, longing to be outdoors.

Kate's mind strayed to the stack of schoolbooks on her half of the bureau at home. Other years, she had brought books along so Mama could help her keep up with her lessons during the months that school was in session. But by the time boating season was over this winter, she would have fallen behind, just like all the other canal boat children. Mama would hate that, because she had vowed that being on the waterway would never interfere with Kate's becoming "a well-educated young lady."

"Well, it will be her own fault," Kate muttered, "hers and that baby's." She wondered if Mama would tell them that Dr. Smith had brought the baby in his black bag. Well, Julia might believe that, but *she* knew better.

The spring before, Kate had watched, fascinated, while Mrs. Steller's Tabby had her kittens in Cupid's stall in the mule shed, and she figured that babies probably arrived in pretty much the same way. Kate had never told anyone that she'd seen the kittens born—she was pretty sure that was another one of the many things that "people don't talk about."

Chapter Five

Minutes later Kate looked ahead to where the canal narrowed to the width of the boat and was enclosed by chest-high walls. The first aqueduct. *An aqueduct is nothing but a bridge to take the canal and towpath across a creek or river, Katie.* That's what Papa had told her when she'd first asked about one of the water-filled stone troughs high above a stream.

Kate saw a boat approaching the aqueduct from the other direction, and she called, "Keep going, Seth! Loaded boats have the right of way." She saw that the light boat was edging toward the berm—the bank opposite the towpath. Good, she thought when its mules stopped and the towline sank to the bottom of the canal. There would be no problem here.

She heard Cupid's and Junior's hooves clatter on the stone walkway as they crossed the aqueduct, saw Seth look over the railing and wave to someone below. Union pickets, probably. Kate had grown used to seeing soldiers in Cumberland, and she knew the army occupied the other towns along the Potomac, too. It made her feel safe to know that Union troops were always close by, protecting the canal and keeping an eye on the river, making sure the Rebels stayed out of Maryland. Or chasing them back to Virginia if they did come—like they had the past September.

Kate refused to think about how the Rebel army had damaged locks and burned boats, how they'd even broken through the canal wall to drain the waterway. Instead, she thought of the map in her geography book, the one that showed the Potomac River forming the boundary between Maryland and Virginia. Between the United States and the Confederacy, now, though western Virginia would soon join the union as the new state of West Virginia.

Two years ago, when Papa was captain and the war was new, Kate had found it exciting to be boating along the very edge of the United States, but she had hardly thought about that last year when she started out with Mama. Now, though, it seemed a little scary.

As the boat left the aqueduct, Kate waved to the driver of the waiting team and the man called, "Didn't have no trouble this trip. There's Federal troops at all the fords and ferry landings."

Reassured, Kate said, "This is going to be a good boating season. Not like the last two, right?"

The man grinned and said, "Let's hope so, missy."

It was well past noon when Kate brought a long, tin horn to her lips, blew three notes, and then hollered, "HE-EY, LOCK!" She grinned at the way Seth nearly jumped out of his skin at the blare of the horn. Watching him, she tried to imagine what he was thinking. She could almost feel him straining his eyes, maybe blinking, wondering why he couldn't see any lock up ahead.

Soon, though, the narrow stone passageway came into view. Kate swallowed hard. This was their first test. She wasn't worried about steering *The Mary Ann* into the lock, but could Seth do his part? Kate became conscious of a dull ache in the back of her head. She relaxed a little when a woman came out of the lock house, wiping her hands on her apron. At least it would be Mrs. Lassen and not her crotchety husband who would lock them through.

"Tee, yip, YA-ah!" Kate called. As the boat drifted toward Seth, she wondered if he knew that their success or failure rested on him, on what he did in the next few minutes. When she saw the uncertain look on his face, Kate's own confidence began to fade. What if Seth fumbled with the line and the boat crashed into the downstream gates?

Refusing to think about that, Kate took a deep breath and said, "Listen carefully so you'll know what to do." She ticked off the steps on her fingers. "Stop the mules so the boat can drift into the lock. Run back so I can throw you the snubbing line—that's a rope attached to the boat. Wind the line around the snubbing post—you'll see a big wooden post—and pull back on it to stop the boat. Don't yank the line—just pull it tight."

Kate paused, and when Seth nodded, she said, "After that, you'll help the lock tender—this time, it will be the lock tender's wife—close the wooden gates behind the boat. Then you'll go back to the snubbing post and take hold of the line while she goes to the other end of the lock."

"And then what?" Seth asked.

"When she hollers 'Lock ready,' you holler back 'Line ready,' and she'll turn a couple of cranks that stick up from the downstream gates. That opens the paddles—little doors at the bottom of the gates—to let the water in the lock drain out and lower the boat to the same level as the canal ahead of us. It's like taking the boat down a step."

When Seth nodded again, Kate continued. "As the water runs out of the lock and the boat goes down, you have to let the line out a little at a time, and last of all, you push open your side of the downstream gates. Don't worry, you can do it."

Kate hoped she sounded more confident than she felt. If Seth let the line out too fast, the boat would be buffeted about by the rushing water and might hit the lock walls, but if he didn't let the line out fast enough, it could break. The snubbing post might even snap off. Kate's headache began to pound.

Seth was staring at the lock ahead of them. "It looks like an awfully tight fit," he said.

"Three inches to spare on each side and a couple of feet front and back," Kate said flatly as she used the pole to push the boat away from the bank. "Let's go." She went back to the tiller and concentrated on the closed down-stream gates at the far end of the lock, sighting across the small American flag at the bow. Carefully, she maneuvered the boat until the tip of the flagstaff pointed at the vertical line where the two strong, watertight gates met. There! She knew she could do it.

Seth was waiting to catch the line, and Kate was certain he was holding his breath as the boat slipped into the lock chamber like a hand into a glove. Now it was all up to him. She tossed her stepbrother the coiled line and watched anxiously as he headed for the snubbing post. After the briefest hesitation, Seth wrapped the line around the post and pulled back on it, bringing the drifting boat to a stop.

Drawing a deep breath, Kate thought, One lock down, seventy-three more to go. *Seventy-three more locks—and the tunnel.* The enormity of what she'd undertaken swept over her, but then she remembered the poem Mama had taught her.

"What was that you said?" Seth asked.

Kate hadn't been aware she'd recited the words aloud. "It's a poem my mother likes," she said, raising her voice so she could be heard over the sound of the water rushing out of the lock. "Part of it goes like this: 'One step and then another, and the longest trip's begun.'" After the two locks within the next quarter mile, there would be only seventy-*one* more, Kate told herself, refusing to think about the tunnel.

Seth looked at her appraisingly and said, "Looks to me like all the steps on this trip are going to be mine. And the mules', of course."

"We'll change the mules when we come to the third lock," Kate said, watching tensely while Seth played out the line as the water level in the lock was lowered. "They'll have shorter shifts since this is the first day out. You aren't tired yet, are you? Remember, you can take your shoes off if you want." Kate knew she wouldn't want to walk all day with shoes on.

"I'm fine," Seth said quickly, but Kate barely heard him. She had turned to watch a cavalry patrol riding upstream. Rebel raiders wouldn't dare bother the boaters this year, she thought with satisfaction.

Suddenly Kate noticed that the lock gates ahead of her had opened and *The Mary Ann* was under way again. Shaken, she muttered, "A captain has to pay attention."

After they had passed through the third of the closely spaced locks, Kate took a deep breath. Seth learned fast, she thought, impressed in spite of herself. And so far at least, he didn't complain. He had to be tired, and even hungrier than she was, since he'd walked so far.

She should have known that to manage with a crew of two, boaters would have to take turns driving the mules and steering, Kate thought. She would love to walk along beside the mules, but she knew her mother would never forgive her if she did.

"You're getting to be a young lady now," Mama had said last year when Kate begged to be allowed to drive the mules so they would have to hire only one boy. Walking on the towpath with Papa when she was younger had been different, Mama said firmly. And it didn't matter to her what other families did—no daughter of hers would be a mule driver, and that was final.

But with only one driver, this trip was going to take longer than ever, Kate thought, frowning. Well, it couldn't be helped, so she might as well stop worrying and enjoy being on the waterway again. Her eyes searched the grassy edge of the towpath for the waxy white blossoms of bloodroot that grew along this stretch, but the thin green spikes of wild onion were the only sign of spring she could find. . . .

After the boat had been lowered to the next level of the canal and Seth was standing above her on the lock wall, coiling the snubbing line, Kate looked up at him and said, "If you step over onto the cabin roof and then down to the tiller deck, we'll have lunch."

"I wondered if we were ever going to eat. But what if another boat comes along?"

"You don't think we're going to sit here in the lock, do you?" Kate raised her voice and called, "COME up, General! COME up, Sandy." Then she turned to Seth. "We'll eat as soon as you go in the cabin and bring out the lunch basket."

"Get the basket yourself. You haven't walked all the way from Cumberland like I have."

How dare he talk to her like that? Keeping her eyes on the straining mules, Kate forced herself to speak calmly. "A crew member never questions the captain's authority," she said. "We'll eat when you bring the basket."

His back stiff, Seth made his way to the cabin, and Kate congratulated herself on having had the last word. Her stomach grumbled, and she wondered what Julia had packed for them. What was taking Seth so long, anyway?

Drumming her fingers on the tiller, Kate waited a little longer and then went into the cabin. To her surprise, her stepbrother was sitting at the table with crumbs and bits of eggshell in front of him and a piece of cake halfway to his mouth.

"What do you think you're doing?" Kate demanded. "You were supposed to bring the lunch outside."

"Your crew has mutinied, captain," Seth said. "Your share is in the basket—cheese sandwiches, hard-boiled eggs, apples, and cake. I don't see what's so important about being the captain, anyway."

"Somebody's got to be in charge, and it has to be me, because I'm the one that knows what to do," Kate said, reaching for an apple.

"What's there to know? Looks to me like the mules walk on the towpath and the boat floats along behind them. It doesn't seem to matter whether anybody's in charge or not."

"That's because I picked a straight stretch for our lunch break. And the mules slow down if somebody isn't there to keep them moving." Kate bit into the apple with a satisfying crunch and felt the spray of sweet juice in her mouth. "Look, it's going to take us a lot longer to get to Georgetown if you don't do your part," she said, trying to sound reasonable. And in a flash of inspiration she added, "Our navy needs this load of coal for its steamships, don't forget."

Brushing the crumbs off his lap, Seth said, "Are you trying to tell me it's my patriotic duty to let you boss me around?"

Kate's eyes blazed. "You're impossible! I wish—"

There was a jolt as the boat drifted too near the bank and scraped the slope of the canal bottom. To Kate's surprise, before she had regained her balance, Seth was on his way out the cabin door. She followed and saw him shove the boat away from the bank with the pole he had used at the wharf. "He thinks he's so smart," she said under her breath as she hurried to the tiller.

"What's the big idea?" Seth hollered when Kate steered into the bank again.

"I want you to get off and drive those mules," she called. When she pulled in the plank and watched him run toward the team she asked herself, If Seth catches on so quickly, how come he doesn't understand by now that he has to do what I tell him? While we're boating, anyway.

It was a good thing she hadn't had to stop to prepare a meal, Kate thought, back at the tiller with the lunch basket at her feet. They weren't making very good time as it was, and no matter what Seth said, he had to be tired. "Hey, Seth," Kate hollered, "you can ride the lead mule if you want to." That might speed them up a little, she thought as she finished her sandwich and cracked the shell of the hard-boiled egg.

Seth didn't answer, but he seemed to make an effort to look more energetic. He wasn't going to let on how tired he was, Kate thought, feeling a grudging respect for her stepbrother.

Chapter Six

Late that afternoon, Kate noticed Seth was limping. How would they ever get to Georgetown if they barely made fifteen miles a day? "Tee, yip, YA-ah!" she called, steering toward the towpath bank. Seth turned to face her, and when Kate saw how tired he looked, she felt a pang of conscience. Fifteen miles might not be a good day's distance for *The Mary Ann*, but it was a very long way for a driver to walk on the first day out.

"We're tying up early," Kate called, gradually bringing the boat closer and closer to the bank until it settled to a stop. After a struggle, she managed to put the heavy mule fall board in place, and Cupid and Junior trotted obediently from the stable to the towpath. Kate followed them down, lugging their feed trough, and noticing Seth's surprised expression she said, "You didn't think we kept the mules on the boat at night, did you? Go get a sack of corn and fill this trough for me."

Silently, he obeyed, and Kate called after him, "You'll have to wipe off the mules' collars and harnesses while I brush them, and after that you can stuff our mattress covers with hay." She lifted the leather traces off the mules' backs and waited while they rolled in the dust of the towpath. Seth must be too tired to care about being ordered around, Kate thought as she brushed General, crooning to him as she worked.

Kate felt Seth's eyes on her and looked up to see him watching. "What's the matter with you?" she asked sharply.

"Nothing. I was just wondering why you can't be half as nice to people as you are to those mules."

Seth's words came as a jolt, but Kate managed to say, "On the waterway, the mules come first." She'd have to make an effort to be nicer, so her stepbrother would have no excuse to say something like that again.

When she finished caring for the mules, Kate went aboard. "I'm going to pole us across the canal to the berm side and tie up there," she said, pulling up the plank, "and while you finish stuffing those mattress covers, I'll get out the canvas so we can put up the awning." That was one of the things they usually did before they left Cumberland. But then, usually they didn't leave in such a hurry.

It seemed to take forever to get the awning in place, and when they finally finished Kate frowned and said, "It isn't supposed to sag like that."

"I'll tighten it up while you start supper," Seth said. Kate went inside, glad her stepbrother hadn't mentioned that he would be driving the mules in all kinds of weather while she was sheltered from the sun and rain.

When Seth came inside a short time later, Kate could tell that he was pleasantly surprised to see how homey the small cabin seemed with the lamp lit and a fire in the stove. "I'm sorry not to have a hot meal for you, but there'll be tea to go with the cookies Mrs. Rollins gave us for dessert."

"That's all right," Seth said, almost falling into his chair. His eyes moved from the wedge of cheese and the bread Kate had sliced to the basket of freshly baked cookies the wife of the last lock tender had given Kate.

"In the summer, we can buy fresh vegetables from the lock tenders' wives, but all they have for sale now is home-baked bread and maybe milk and butter," Kate said as she unscrewed the lid from a jar of milk and poured it into their glasses.

Seth frowned. "How did you pay for that bread and milk, anyway?"

"I took half the money Mama had in the sugar bowl," Kate said, "and don't look so shocked—I told her so in the letter I wrote. It takes money to make money, don't forget." That was what Papa always said, Kate added silently, turning back to the stove.

"Here," she said after she poured hot water from the kettle into a basin and tested its temperature with her hand. "Soak your feet in this." Seth looked so surprised she couldn't resist saying, "You see, I can be nice to people, too."

As Seth peeled off his socks and gingerly lowered his feet into the steaming water he said, "You just want to make sure I'll be able to walk again tomorrow."

Kate frowned as she measured out tea leaves and poured boiling water into the teapot. He'd better be able to walk tomorrow, she thought, scooping dried beans into a large cast-iron pot. "There," she said after she had filled the pot with cold water from the keg by the door. "Those beans will soak all night, and I'll cook us some soup for tomorrow."

"For tomorrow, or forever? There's just the two of us, you know."

"For forever, then," Kate said shortly. "Bean soup is very nourishing." Once it was made, she could heat it up every noon and evening, and when it was gone, she'd make another pot. Other than oatmeal, it was all she knew how to cook.

Seth looked up from his tea when a long beam of light shone through the window and fell across the table, and Kate explained, "A boat's passing us—that's the light from its bow lamp. Most folks don't stop this early, and if they've got a big enough crew, they keep going all night, six hours on, six hours off, all the way to Georgetown. Those captains make the most money, but Papa always tied up at night." Her voice faded away.

"You still miss him, don't you? I know you hated it when my father took his place."

"Nobody could ever take his place," Kate said, setting down her teacup. "Especially not your father. Not a singing teacher."

Seth stood up, obviously struggling to control himself. "I've had all I can take of you," he said. "I'm going to bed now, and in the morning, I'm going home." He limped toward the door, leaving a trail of wet footprints.

She'd gone too far. "Wait, Seth!" Kate called after him. But when he stopped in the doorway and looked back at her, she was shaken by the dark anger in his eyes. "You'll need some blankets," she said lamely. She found the ones she'd packed and held two of them out to him.

Seth took them from her without a word and went out into the darkness. Kate stared after him. Now what was she going to do? There was no way she could manage alone—she'd have to think of some way to keep Seth from leaving. He'd never once complained that he was tired, and he'd managed the snubbing lines with no trouble at all.

Suddenly aware of how tired she was, Kate decided to go to bed early and leave the dishes until morning. But as she lay under her blankets and the quilt she'd helped Mama piece, she found herself thinking about Seth shivering in the unheated hay house, probably too angry to sleep.

She shouldn't have said what she did about his father, especially when Seth was trying to be nice, Kate thought. She didn't blame him for being angry with her, but he had no right to use that as an excuse to go home. If he went home tomorrow morning—

But he wouldn't, Kate realized, because he'd never be able to face her mother if he did. Besides, the last thing her stepfather had said to Seth before he went off to war was, "You'll be the man of the house while I'm gone, son, and I expect you to take care of your mother and sisters." He would stay to "take care of" her!

Kate's relief that Seth would stay with *The Mary Ann* was almost overshadowed by the resentment she felt at the memory of his father's words. She wasn't Seth's sister, and Mama wasn't his mother, and they never would be. Saying something didn't make it so any more than wishing something did. If wishing made a difference, Seth and Julia would disappear from her life, just as her stepfather had when he left to fight the Rebels.

"But not right now," she said aloud in the darkness. Much as she hated to admit it, she needed them both in order to carry out her plan. "But I don't need *him*," she muttered resentfully, meaning her stepfather. She didn't see why her mother needed him, either. Mama had told her she'd understand when she was older, but Kate didn't know what there was to understand.

It was too complicated to think about. Right now, the

only thing that mattered was getting their boatload of coal to Georgetown and collecting their pay. Kate closed her eyes and burrowed deeper into her blankets, trying to forget how many miles lay ahead of them, trying to still the echo of what Seth had said the night before: *Two* men, *Kate. Not a boy my age and a girl.*

Chapter Seven

Shivering in the morning cold, Kate added some corn-cobs to the embers of last night's fire. Seth can bring in a scuttle of coal to keep that going, she thought as she opened the small compartment below the waterline that served as an icebox.

After hesitating for a moment with the jar of milk in her hand, Kate went to the shelf for Mama's blue pitcher. "There," she said, looking at the small table with approval for a moment before she headed for the hay house.

She paused outside the door, then knocked and called, "Are you dressed? I need to get corn for the mules."

"I'm dressed," Seth said, and when Kate went inside, blinking in the dim light, he was sitting on the edge of his bunk staring down at his feet. Kate's eyes widened when she saw how blistered and swollen they were, and she couldn't help saying, "I guess you won't be walking back to Cumberland today after all."

Seth stood up, wincing. "I'd already decided to stay," he said.

"I should have told you that you did a good job yesterday," Kate said as she busied herself with gathering up ears of corn. She should have insisted that he walk barefoot, too. As she left the hay house she said, "I'll fix a basin of hot water for your feet."

When Seth hobbled into the cabin a short time later and slowly lowered himself into a chair, Kate said, "Looks like your legs ache, too. After breakfast, I'll show you how to work the tiller."

"You're going to let me steer?" Seth sounded incredulous.

"Well, you're in no shape to drive the mules," Kate said, scraping the last of the oatmeal into their bowls.

"You mean *you're* going to drive them? But you can't!"

"I don't see why not," Kate said, unable to meet his eyes as she sat down at the table opposite him.

"Your mother wouldn't think it's a proper thing for a girl to do, that's why not. She wouldn't like it at all."

Kate's shoulders sagged and she said, "I know. But I can't think of anything else to do. Without a driver, the team just pokes along."

"I'll ride on the lead mule," Seth said reluctantly.

"Thanks," Kate said, even though she knew he was doing it for Mama and not for her. When they had finished their oatmeal, she put the bowls and spoons into the dishpan with the plates from the night before. She added coal to the stove to keep the fire burning and gave a stir to the beans that had soaked overnight. "There," she said. "By lunchtime, that will be bean soup. You can pole us over to the towpath whenever you're ready."

Kate had been surprised to find how hard it was to pole a loaded boat—much harder than it looked when Papa or the hired boys did it. She watched Seth push the pole

49

against the berm to move the boat into the channel of the canal and then dig the pole into the muddy bottom. The pole bent as he leaned his weight on it, and the boat moved slowly toward the grassy bank. Kate scowled. It wasn't fair that boys were so much stronger.

She went ashore to harness the mules, and Seth painfully made his way off the boat. "Here," Kate said, lacing her fingers together, "I'll give you a leg up. Come *on*, Seth, it's the only way."

After she put the other team in the stable, Kate took her place at the tiller, frowning when she saw how stiff and awkward Seth looked, riding on Cupid. Under different circumstances, she might have enjoyed her stepbrother's discomfort, but now she had to depend on him.

A chain was only as strong as its weakest link—that's what Papa always said. "Seth's the weak link, and I'm the chain," Kate whispered, pleased. But her pleasure faded as the meaning of the saying began to sink in. Without Seth, her own skill and experience were about as much use as a length of broken chain.

When they reached the first of the locks at Oldtown, Kate watched Seth slide awkwardly from Cupid's back, wincing when his feet hit the ground and almost stumbling as he moved toward the snubbing post. He didn't complain, and he tried to hide his misery, but it was obvious that Seth was mighty uncomfortable.

Papa had never worked a lame mule, and it must be the same with a boy. Seth needed a couple of days to rest up, and if he didn't get it he wasn't going to be much use for the rest of the trip. There was no way around it, Kate decided—she would have to drive the mules. But not until after they passed through the next two locks, both within a half mile or so, and left the canal-side village behind them.

Actually, Kate thought as the boat began to move slowly out of the lock, driving the mules would be a nice change from steering. Other years, she hadn't been alone at the tiller. Either Papa or Mama had been with her on the tiller deck, and it was a sociable time, not lonely like it was now. She and Papa would sing every song they knew, and Mama would quiz her on the names of the states and their capitals or whatever lesson she had been working on that day, and then the two of them would talk.

If only there were a way for her to drive the mules without upsetting Mama. Kate caught her breath. Maybe there *was* a way! She thought of how miserable Seth looked riding on Cupid, of how he had limped from the snubbing post to the lock gate. Before long he'd agree to just about anything if it meant he wouldn't have to ride Cupid, and if he could ease his painful feet and sore legs.

For the next half hour, Kate steered automatically as she made her plans. She barely noticed the milk wagon on the road along the berm or the sound of the blacksmith's hammer, and she didn't even glance toward the Union fort on the far side of town.

By the time they reached the third Oldtown lock, Kate was ready. "Hey, Seth," she called after he had helped open the downstream gates, "I need you on board—the mules can walk on their own for a time."

Seth joined her at the tiller, and Kate hollered for the team to start. Turning to her stepbrother, she said, "I want you to steer for a while. All you have to do is remember that the tiller moves the rudder, and the rudder changes the boat's direction. Just rest your arm along the tiller and either pull it or push it, depending on which way you need to move to stay in the middle of the waterway. This is a straight stretch with no boats in sight, so go ahead and practice till you get the feel of it."

Seth's voice followed Kate as she ducked into the cabin. "First she makes a big fuss about how she has to be the captain, and now she acts like steering the boat's as easy as pie." Being captain was more than steering, Kate thought scornfully. Seth didn't even know enough to realize that.

After she found the scissors on the top shelf, Kate took off her bonnet and stood in front of the small mirror that hung on the wall. "I can't do it," she whispered to her reflection. But she had to do it. There wasn't any other way.

Catching up a handful of honey-colored hair, Kate brought the scissors so close that she could feel their cold-ness on her neck. She clenched her teeth and began to cut. The scrunch-and-snick of the scissors made her stom-ach turn, and she nearly cried out when the severed tresses wrapped around her hand, almost like a living thing. But she steeled herself, separated out another section of hair, and raised the scissors again.

When she was finally finished, Kate gazed mournfully at the mass of curls lying around her feet. Mama had loved brushing her hair, Kate remembered, almost feeling the tingle of bristles on her scalp and Mama's light touch as her hand smoothed the flyaway hairs that rose to follow the brush. "I did it for you, Mama," Kate whispered as she dropped to her knees to scoop up the tangled locks. She pressed them to her cheek and said, "Now you won't be embarrassed because your daughter's a mule driver."

Kate carried her shorn tresses to the table where she combed them with her fingers and twisted them into a thick skein, which she put on the top shelf. And then she peered in the mirror. The shock Kate felt at the sight of her mangled haircut was quickly followed by disappoint-ment that she still didn't look much like a boy. "Maybe I will once I've got on Seth's clothes," she muttered as she wrapped her shawl around her shorn head and her shoulders. She slipped out of the cabin and headed toward the hay house.

That must be where he keeps his extra things, Kate thought when she saw the flour sack on Seth's bunk. She hesitated a moment, knowing how offended she would be if her stepbrother rummaged through her personal belongings. But this was different, she reminded herself. She had a good reason for what she was about to do.

Kate had pulled out a pair of trousers and a vest, and she was reaching for a shirt when she felt the boat turn sharply toward the berm and then change course and head for the towpath bank. Good, she thought as she slipped out of her dress and petticoat. Seth finally felt confident enough to experiment with the tiller.

"These buttons are on the wrong side," Kate complained as she fastened Seth's shirt. Awkwardly, she stepped into his trousers, tucked in the shirttail, and—blushing a little—did up the trouser buttons. All she was missing was a pair of suspenders, and the vest would hide their absence.

Seth was still experimenting with the tiller when Kate edged along the race plank to join him and said, "I need your cap."

His mouth fell open and he exclaimed, "You've cut off all your hair—and you've got on my clothes! What's the big idea?"

"Stop staring and give me your cap," Kate said, enjoying his reaction. "The idea is that when I'm driving the mules nobody will know I'm a girl, and Mama won't have to be embarrassed," she said, setting the cap on her head at a jaunty angle.

"I can't believe you cut off all your hair," Seth said. "It was so—" He hesitated and then he finished lamely, "—so long."

Now maybe he understood just how serious she was about this trip, how determined she was to make it succeed. "Steer toward the bank so I can go ashore," Kate said, turning away from him.

"You'd better let me even up that haircut for you first. The back is really ragged, and it looks strange under the cap."

He wasn't going to give her an argument! Kate checked to make sure the waterway ahead of them was straight and no boats were in sight, then led the way into the cabin. As she reached for Mama's scissors she said, "If anybody asks, I'm Nate, and we're brothers hired on as crew. Mama—call her Mrs. Hillerman and say she used to be Mrs. Betts—is in bed because she doesn't feel well, and Kate's inside looking after her."

Kate looked in the mirror again and saw that Seth's shirt and cap made her look more boyish, and she adjusted her expression into one she thought was masculine.

"Stop making faces and bring me those scissors," Seth said.

Embarrassed, Kate draped a dish towel around her neck and sat down in front of him. Her skin crawled as the cold metal of the scissors touched her neck, and she hoped Seth wouldn't nick her ear.

While Seth trimmed, Kate said reluctantly, "I guess I'd better teach you how to lock through so I don't have to keep getting on and off the boat. We don't want to do anything to draw attention to ourselves." She explained how to sight over the flagstaff on the bow, making it line up with the center of the lock gates, so he could hold the boat on course.

"That's all there is to it?"

"Except for throwing me the snubbing line," Kate said. "You'd better not forget that, 'cause if you do, we'll crash through the downstream gates and wash down to the next level."

Waving aside her warning, Seth scoffed, "And you told me how you had to be the captain because you were the one who knew what to do! From now on, we'll both be captains." He put down the scissors and lifted the towel from Kate's shoulders.

With great effort, she kept her voice even. "No, we'll both steer the boat and we'll both drive the mules, but there can only be one captain. One person has to be in charge, and I'm more experienced, even if you have been on the canal for more than a day now. So I'm the captain. I make the decisions, and you have to go along with them."

"Now look, Kate, that's hardly fair. If it weren't for me, you wouldn't be able to make this trip, and—"

"Every captain needs a crew. And no matter what you do on this trip, that's all you'll ever be—crew. Now, go on out and steer toward the bank so I can get off and drive the mules."

"Aye, aye, sir!" Seth said, giving Kate a mock salute on his way out of the cabin. As he leaned on the tiller to bring the boat toward the bank he mimicked, " 'That's all you'll ever be—crew.' "

She'd tried to be nice to Seth, and look what happened, Kate thought as she ran to catch up to the mules. She never should have said he could steer the boat through the locks—it had given him a swelled head. He'd never dared to mock her like that before. "He shouldn't be surprised if I'm nicer to you mules than I am to him," she said, resting her hand on Junior's neck. "None of you ever mock me—or want to be captain." Kate smiled at the thought, and she began to feel a little better.

Chapter Eight

So this is what it's like to be a boy, Kate thought as she walked along beside the mules. No bonnet blocking your vision. No skirts twisting about your ankles. She raised her face to the sun and lengthened her stride. It felt a bit strange to be wearing trousers, but it was wonderful!

Kate savored the feel of the cool dirt under her bare feet, glad the day had warmed up. She waved to a farmer who was walking behind his horse, plowing the rich, dark soil on the flat between the canal and the river, and she breathed in the primitive scent of freshly turned earth. How could anyone stand to live in a city or town the whole year long?

Suddenly, Kate's eyes fell on a patch of spring beauties blooming in the grass at the edge of the towpath, their pale petals delicately striped with pink, and a wave of sadness washed over her. Each year when Papa found the first of the tiny blossoms, he had stopped the boat so she and Mama could come ashore to admire them. He would reach into his pocket and bring out a bag of peppermint drops, and then he would remind them that when his Katie was little, she had thought the flowers looked like peppermint candy.

"I miss you so much, Papa," Kate whispered, blinking back tears. How could Mama have forgotten him so soon?

This time last year, Mama still missed him, Kate remembered. Last year, she and Mama had clung to each other and wept when they found the first patch of spring beauties. And then, unable to enjoy the peppermint drops Mama had brought, they gave them to the hired drivers. "A year ago Mama still missed him," Kate whispered, "and now she's married to somebody else. Now she's having somebody else's baby."

Realizing that the mules had slowed, Kate said, "COME up! COME up, you two." Ahead of her, the towpath curved to follow the riverbank again, and she knew they were approaching the next lock. She began to feel uneasy as she neared the sharp turn in the towpath, knowing that as she rounded it she would see the lock ahead of her. Besides being Seth's first attempt at locking through, this would be a real test of her disguise, since the elderly lock tender was a special friend of hers and loved to tease her.

Kate gave a start when she heard Seth blow a spluttery blast on the horn, and she had to smile in spite of her nervousness when after another feeble attempt he gave up and simply yelled, "HE-EY, LOCK!" She'd have to tell him to keep his lips almost closed when he pressed them against the mouthpiece. But first, they had to get through this lock.

With every step that took her closer to the narrow passageway, Kate grew more tense. After she stopped the mules and ran back, ready to catch the snubbing line, she stood and watched helplessly as *The Mary Ann*'s bow moved slowly toward the lock. Kate held her breath, willing Seth to steer safely between its walls.

He'd done it! Kate remembered how terrified she'd been the first time she'd locked through, and Papa had been beside her at the tiller, reassuring her every bit of the way, ready to take over if she needed him. But Seth had done it alone, and on his first day as steersman, too.

Kate's heart beat faster as she caught the coiled rope he tossed to her. She'd never snubbed a line before. Well, she'd watched other boaters do it often enough, she told herself sternly, and if Seth could do it, she should certainly be able to. She looped the line around the snubbing post and pulled back on it to bring the drifting boat to a stop.

Getting a better grip on the line, Kate told herself that all she had to do now was slowly play out the line while the water level in the lock was lowered. She was glad that this was one of the lock tenders who insisted on managing the gates by himself unless another boat was waiting.

"First time you tried that, sonny?" the old man asked Kate, pausing beside her. She nodded, and he said, "You wrap the line around your hand like that, and it might be the last time you do it for a while."

Kate knew her face was red with embarrassment as she awkwardly held the line taut with her left hand while she changed the grip with her right. She tried not to think of how the rough rope might have torn her skin. She should have known better!

"Where's Miz Betts, sonny?" the lock tender asked, his gaze shifting to the boat. "And where's that little gal of hers?"

"She's Miz Hillerman now, and she's feeling poorly lately," Kate replied, pleased that she hadn't been recognized. "Her daughter's in the cabin with her. Me and my brother's managin' the boat for 'em, but he's a lot better at drivin' mules than he is at the tiller."

"Looked to me like he done all right just now," the old man said as he headed toward the downstream gate.

"You have your nerve, telling him I'm no good at the tiller!" Seth said. "What's the big idea?"

"At least I said it right in front of you instead of when I figured you couldn't hear me," Kate retorted. She heard the call "Lock ready" and called back, "Line ready!" She could do this. She *had* to do it.

Above the sound of the rushing water Seth said stiffly, "I shouldn't have mocked you, whether I thought you were listening or not."

He hadn't said he was sorry, but at least he'd had the grace to admit he was wrong. "Well," Kate said, carefully playing out the snubbing line, "see that you don't do it again."

Seth had steered the boat into the lock as if he'd been doing it all his life, Kate thought uneasily. She'd have to make sure it didn't go to his head.

When Kate saw the aqueduct ahead, she stopped the mules and ran back to the boat, calling, "Set out the plank!"

Once on board, she said, "An aqueduct's a lot harder than a lock, 'cause there's nothing to sight on." At the tiller again, she hollered to the mules and steered the boat into the center of the waterway, easing the stick one way and then the other until she was certain the boat was centered. As her hand relaxed, she noticed that Seth had been watching her every move.

"So what do you do, imagine gates at the far end and steer toward where they would meet in the center?"

Kate nodded. "That's how Papa taught me to do it," she said. But Seth had figured it out for himself!

"Then I can steer us through if we come to another aqueduct while I'm captain," he said.

"When you're *steersman*," Kate said. Keeping her eyes on the place where the imaginary gates met she said, "You're either the steersman or the mule driver, depending on what job you have at the moment, but I'm the captain no matter what I'm doing. Sometimes I'll be steering, and sometimes I'll be driving the mules, but I'll always be the captain."

The bow of the boat entered the narrow aqueduct and Kate turned to her stepbrother and asked, "Do you understand that?"

"Perfectly. I understand that you like to lord it over me every chance you get."

Kate was stunned by the resentment she saw in her stepbrother's eyes. "Well then, don't give me the chance to," she said, trying to sound reasonable. "Just accept the fact that I'm the captain, and I won't ever have to remind you again. That's what you call 'lording it over you,' isn't it—reminding you that I'm captain?"

For a moment, only the clopping of the mule's hooves on the stone of the aqueduct broke the silence, but then Seth said, "It's more *how* you remind me, like you really enjoy putting me in my place."

Kate didn't know what to say to that. It wasn't so much that she enjoyed it, she just didn't know any other way to keep him from taking over *her* place. Finally she said, "What I really do enjoy is being here on the waterway again, but I'd enjoy it a lot more if you weren't always trying to take over."

Scowling, Seth said, "I'm not used to having a girl order me around."

"Then don't think of me as a girl—just think of me as the captain. That ought to be easier now that I don't look like a girl anymore."

60

"You don't look much like a captain, either," Seth retorted.

At least he wasn't scowling anymore, Kate thought. "Well, you look like a good enough steersman to take us through the aqueducts when you're at the tiller," she said, "but right now I need you to haul in the plank after I go ashore."

On the towpath again, Kate saw a flash of color and watched a cardinal fly across the canal and alight in a tree on the wooded hillside rising from the berm. His clear, liquid call filled the air and was echoed by another in the distance. Glancing back, Kate saw that Seth was watching something in the field that stretched along the floodplain between the towpath and the river. She followed his gaze and saw that a flock of robins had landed on the recently turned soil.

Lunch, Kate thought as one of the birds tugged at a worm, and suddenly she realized that the sun was high overhead. "COME up! COME up!" Kate urged, and the mule team obediently picked up speed. Far ahead, Kate could see the next lock. "Good," she said. "We'll pull in and change the teams, and then I'll go aboard and fix our noon meal."

Kate was ravenously hungry by the time they had locked through, and she was thankful that the next level started with a straight stretch where the boat could float freely while they had their midday meal in the cabin. Once the boat was under way, Kate said, "Let's eat—I'm half starved." As she reached for her apron she announced, "You know, I just might decide to stay a boy."

"Boys don't wear aprons," Seth said, limping to his place at the table. "And they take off their caps when they go inside."

Kate grinned as she tied her apron, and she didn't take

off the cap. "So how do you like steering the boat?" she asked as she turned to ladle up bowls of piping-hot bean soup.

"Fine, but I'd rather drive the mules."

"So would I," Kate agreed as she carried the bowls to the table. "Once your feet are better, we'll take turns."

Seth didn't argue. "Good. Half a day of walking is enough for me," he said.

"We're already way behind schedule," Kate said, thinking guiltily of their late start that day. She was used to having Mama wake her each morning.

" 'Slow but steady often wins the race,' don't forget," Seth reminded her.

Kate carefully cut another slice of bread. "It sounds like you've decided we're going to make it," she said.

"I wasn't so sure at first," Seth admitted.

"But you're sure now?"

His eyes on Kate's cap, he said, "I'm positive."

A wave of relief swept over Kate—relief and gratitude. But all she said was, "Well, it'll be a lot easier with you on my side instead of against me."

"Now, wait a minute," Seth objected. *"You're* the one who's always been against *me.* You've been against me—and Julia, too—from the very first, and you never made any secret of it."

Kate's face felt hot, and she knew she was blushing. "Well, it was nothing personal," she said, not meeting his eyes. She finished her soup and slid the bowl into the dishpan, wrinkling her nose in distaste at the sight of the cold, scummy water.

It had been good to rest for a little while, Kate thought as she left the cabin. Seth was right—half a day of walking was enough. Maybe even more than enough.

Chapter Nine

By midafternoon, it was unseasonably warm. The towpath was dusty now instead of cool under Kate's feet, and the season's first gnats were hovering around her. Perspiration dripped down her face, and Seth's shirt stuck damply to her back.

The bare branches of the trees growing on the flood-plain between the canal and river gave no real shade, but their trunks cast linear shadows across the towpath. The alternating stripes of light and dark seemed to waver as Kate approached them, and she felt queasy.

The blast of a horn startled her, and she looked back to see that they were being overtaken. She stopped the mules on the river side of the towpath and gestured for Seth to steer toward the berm. Half embarrassed that they were going slowly enough to be passed and half glad for the chance to rest, Kate stood beside Sandy and waited.

The other team's driver was a long-legged young man,

and he spoke cheerfully as he went by. The boat—a brand-new one by the looks of it—passed over *The Mary Ann's* towline, and the captain raised a hand in greeting as he glided past Kate. Yes, it was a new boat, she thought when she saw *The Falling Star* written in script across the stern.

"COME up, Sandy! COME up, General!" Kate commanded, and the mules stepped forward smartly. "COME up, boys," she urged, determined to make better time. "Let's keep up the pace." But no matter how fast Kate walked, the other boat continued to outdistance them. *Two men, Kate. Not a boy my age and a girl.*

Seth had been right, Kate thought, slowing down a little to ease the stitch in her side. This was their second day out, but those men had probably left Cumberland that very morning. "They'll pass us coming back before we're halfway to Georgetown, at this rate," she grumbled. And they would be at the tunnel in no time at all. In spite of the sun beating down on her, Kate felt a chill.

"Tee, yip, YA-ah!"

Kate stopped the mules and looked back at Seth, envying him the shelter of the canvas awning. She wiped the perspiration from her face and wondered how it could be this hot in April.

"You'd better not overdo it in this heat, Kate. You need a straw hat if you're going to be out in the sun all day."

"It really is hot, and the gnats are just awful," Kate said, waving them away. But when she remembered that Seth hadn't said a single word of complaint the day before she added, "You were lucky that yesterday was cool and breezy."

"We'd be in a fine fix if neither one of us could drive the mules tomorrow," Seth said.

He was right, Kate thought, and swallowing her pride she said, "I guess we should tie up early, then."

"Either that or you come aboard and let the mules walk on their own."

"It's hot for them, too, don't forget," Kate said quickly. "We'll tie up here." That way she wouldn't have to face the tunnel until tomorrow.

Once the extra team was unloaded from the stable, Seth said, "I'll take care of the mules while you rest. You don't look so good, Kate."

I don't feel so good, either, Kate answered silently. She felt light-headed, and she ached from her ankles to her hips. "I'll be fine as soon as I have a dipper of water and wash my face," she said. But once she was inside, she didn't want to leave the cabin's cool dimness. The bed in the corner seemed to beckon to her, and she whispered, "I'll lie down for just a minute."

The next thing Kate knew, it was dark. How long had she slept? And where was Seth? Shivering in the cool night air, Kate dragged herself out of bed and wrapped her shawl around her shoulders. As she walked stiffly to the door she wondered how the temperature could have dropped so much since afternoon—and how a day of walking on level ground could make her ache so.

"What are you doing out here?" Kate asked when she opened the cabin door and saw Seth sitting on the race plank.

"Wondering when you were going to get up and fix supper. Are you feeling better?"

Kate nodded. "I'm fine now," she said, "and if you bring me some corncobs, I'll start the fire."

"We could have bread and cheese again instead of heating up the soup."

Kate thought of the dishpan full of bowls and cutlery and said, "All right, but we'll still need a fire to heat some water." Inside again, she used the last clean knife to slice the bread and cheese and then poured their milk into cups because all the glasses were dirty. Setting the table with saucers for plates, Kate glanced at the scummy dishpan and wrinkled her nose in distaste. No wonder Mama insisted that dishes must be washed as soon as a meal was over.

Seth came in and built a fire using the corncobs for fuel, and Kate put a kettle of water on the stove to heat.

"For tea?" Seth asked, his voice hopeful.

"For washing dishes."

Much later Kate said, "I'll need more coal to keep the stove going overnight." When Seth didn't respond, she asked sharply, "Can you get it for me, please?"

"I'll get it in a little while. Right now, I'm going to soak my feet again," Seth said, filling a basin with the last of the hot water.

Kate narrowed her eyes but said nothing. He probably didn't like it that she slept snug and warm in the cabin while he froze on his bunk in the hay house, she thought. The long beam from a bow lamp cut through the darkness outside the window, and Kate heard the crack of a whip followed by a shouted, "COME up, you fool critters! COME up! COME up!"

"Now do you see why I didn't want to rent out the boat and our teams?" Kate asked. "Men like that one run their animals right into the ground," she said grimly. "River scum, that's what he is."

"He sounds drunk," Seth said, frowning.

Another voice shouted for the driver to stop his team, and Kate flinched when he in turn unleashed a stream of abuse at the mules. Glancing at Seth, she saw that he didn't like it any more than she did that the other crew was tying up so close to them. Tying up early because they were too drunk to manage that tricky exit from the tunnel, most likely.

"You never know what drunks might do," she said, trying to put the tunnel out of her mind. "We'd better close the shutters, 'cause those men will be less likely to come back here if they don't see our light."

Seth dried his feet. "I'll close them now," he said as a burst of angry voices broke the silence.

"Get the coal while you're out there, and hurry," Kate said, handing him the scuttle. She heard him fasten all the shutters, heard him lift a hatch cover and fill the scuttle with coal, heard him replace the hatch cover. She finished drying the dishes she had washed, but still Seth didn't come inside. What was keeping him?

Kate opened the door and saw the scuttle filled with coal, but nothing else. "Seth!" she hissed. "Are you out there?"

A torrent of curses came from the other boat, and Kate grabbed the heavy scuttle and retreated to the cabin. She pulled the door shut again and leaned against it, her heart racing. The lamp flickered, casting strange shadows, and the cabin no longer seemed cozy, or even familiar. It wasn't the safe place she knew from other years at all.

She gave a start when she heard a thumping noise outside, a noise that sounded like something—or somebody—was being dragged across the boat. If only Papa were here to protect her! She had never been afraid when he was here—not even once. She'd never been afraid last year with Mama, either. Except, of course, when they heard that the Rebel army was headed for Maryland. Everybody on the waterway was afraid then.

Kate pressed herself against the wall and waited, terrified, as the sound grew louder. If someone pushed the door open, she'd be out of sight behind it, but what would she do if—

"Open the door, Kate."

She yanked it open and gasped, "Where did you go? And what's that you have there?"

"My mattress and blankets," Seth said, answering her second question. "I didn't like the idea of you spending the night alone in the cabin with those drunks so close."

He probably didn't like the idea of shivering in the hay house another night, either, Kate thought. But she was so glad to see him that all she said was, "Make up your bed over there against the wall, so it won't be in the way."

Kate poured coal into the stove and then sat down at the table with the long hank of hair she'd cut off that morning. Maybe if she kept busy, she wouldn't worry about the drunks.

"What are you going to do with all that hair?" Seth asked in surprise when he joined her.

"I'm going to braid it and sew the plaits to the back of my sunbonnet, so I can look like a girl if I want to. Here, hold this for me."

Gingerly, Seth took the ends of the long tendrils Kate handed him.

"Go on, it won't bite you," she said impatiently. "Hold it tight, now." She worked quickly, leaving several inches of hair loose to curl. After she had finished the second braid, Kate threaded the needle she'd found stuck into a spool on the shelf by the scissors and set to work attaching the braids to her bonnet.

"How's this?" she asked at last, trying it on.

"The front looks different than before, but it's fine."

Kate took the small mirror from the wall and carried it closer to the oil lamp. "Who says you can't have your cake and eat it, too?" she asked. The warmth of the small cabin made her yawn, and as she took off the bonnet she said, "I guess it must be bedtime."

"I guess."

After an awkward pause Kate said, "If we sleep in our clothes, we won't have to dress in the morning."

"Tsk, tsk," Seth clucked as he limped over to his mattress and began to unfold his blankets. "Sleeping in your clothes, not washing the dishes till there aren't any left, cutting off your hair—what are things coming to!"

Kate blew out the lamp and said, "I don't know what they're coming to, but I know where they're headed—to Georgetown."

"To Georgetown!" Seth echoed her words. It sounded almost like a cheer, Kate thought when she heard the ring of determination in his voice. She knew that Seth had gone along with her plan only because she'd left him no choice, but now he seemed to be as caught up in it as she was.

The coals settled in the belly of the stove with a comfortable sound, and the water lapped gently against the sides of the boat. Kate thought of Mama and asked, "Do you suppose my mother is very angry with me?" As soon as she spoke the words, Kate regretted them. Why had she given her stepbrother the perfect opportunity to point out what a terrible daughter she was?

But when Seth's voice came across the darkness, all he said was, "She doesn't strike me as the kind of woman who gets angry, but she's probably worried."

"Worried!" Kate scoffed. "Why on earth would she worry? There's nothing to worry about along the canal."

"Well, a while ago you were pretty worried about those drunks."

Kate wished Seth hadn't reminded her about the other crew. She raised herself on one elbow and listened for a moment. "I don't hear them, so I guess they must be sleep-ing it off," she said, lying down again. "There is one thing I'm worried about, though," she said, her words coming in a rush.

"Just one?" Seth prompted.

"Uh-huh. The tunnel." Her voice was hardly a whisper.

"What tunnel is that?" Seth asked sleepily.

"*The* tunnel. There's only one. Paw Paw Tunnel takes the canal through a mountain while the river makes a big loop around it."

His voice alert now, Seth echoed, "Through a mountain? Just how long is this tunnel?"

"Almost three quarters of a mile, and it takes forever to get through it." Kate bit her lip, hating the way her voice trembled.

Seth whistled. "It must be pretty dark in there."

"Uh-huh. You have to light your bow lamp. And the mules' hooves echo terribly." Miserable, Kate told herself it was better for Seth to know ahead of time, better than having him find out when they got there tomorrow. But he still didn't know the worst part of all.

In a moment, Seth asked, "So is it the dark or the echo that scares you?"

Why, he was talking to her the way he talked to Julia, Kate thought, not liking it at all but grateful that he hadn't belittled her fear. "It's just being in there," she said, trying to sound matter-of-fact, "being under a mountain and knowing that I'll be there for a long time."

After a moment Kate added, "We'll come to the tunnel first thing in the morning, and since you'll find out anyway, I might as well tell you now. The only way I can get through it is to stay in the cabin." She scarcely breathed as she waited for Seth's reaction.

"Couldn't we let the mules find their way while I steer?" he asked.

He hadn't made fun of her! "The problem is, the mules don't like the tunnel either, and unless somebody leads them, they won't go."

Seth was silent for a moment. "If the tunnel's straight enough, maybe we could just let *The Mary Ann* float through while I drive the mules," he said at last.

"It's pretty straight, and it has wooden bumpers on both sides so no harm's done if the boat scrapes the edge, but what about your feet?"

"I think I can do it if I walk barefooted," he said. "Now try to sleep."

That was easy enough for him to say, Kate thought. She made her mind blank so she wouldn't think about the tunnel, wouldn't worry about the drunks on the boat tied up around the curve. Unpleasantly aware of her bone-deep weariness, she reminded herself that at least her feet weren't blistered.

Outside, Cupid brayed, and Kate sat up in bed. "Seth! Somebody's coming," she whispered. "It must be one of the drunks."

Before Seth could answer, a man yelled, "Hey, on the boat! You got any whiskey?"

"Don't answer, Kate," Seth whispered.

Kate knew there was no way the man could come aboard, since he was on the towpath and they were tied up along the berm, but that didn't keep her heart from pounding.

"Hey! Wake up in there an' gimme some whiskey!"

Cupid brayed again, and the man cursed and said, "Git outta my way, you worthless piece of mule flesh, you."

Without thinking, Kate leaped out of bed and headed

for the door. But Seth was there ahead of her, blocking her way. "Stay here. I'll deal with him."

Taken aback by the authority in her stepbrother's voice, Kate hesitated a moment before she followed him onto the tiller deck. They were in this together, after all. And besides, she was the captain.

"There's no whiskey on this boat, mister," Seth said. "Go on back to your friends."

Raising his lantern, the man looked at Seth and then spat on the ground. "Lemme talk to your captain, boy," he growled.

"Captain's sick, mister," Seth said. "We think it might be typhoid."

"Typhoid!" The man backed up a few steps. "Me mates ain't gonna like it if I don't bring 'em back some whiskey," he said, sounding uncertain.

"They'll like it even less if you bring 'em back typhoid," Seth said.

The man lowered his lantern and stumbled down the towpath toward his boat, muttering as he went. Kate and Seth waited until the bobbing circle of light disappeared, and then they went inside.

"I see that you're a pretty good liar, too," Kate said after she climbed back into bed. "Hey, that was supposed to be a compliment!" she added when her words were followed by stony silence. "You did a good job out there, Seth."

"I couldn't think of any other way to get rid of him," Seth said, sounding apologetic.

"Nobody could possibly blame you for lying to that drunk, Seth. You *had* to lie. Just like I had to lie to Mr. McLain yesterday."

After a moment Seth said, "I guess you're right, Kate. And I don't really blame you for lying to him—I just don't want you lying to me. I don't want to have to wonder whether you're telling me the truth."

Now it was Kate who was silent. Frowning, she thought, We don't have to like each other, but we ought to be able to trust each other. "That's fair enough," she said. "Let's agree that we'll always tell each other the truth."

"Agreed. And now let's try to get some sleep."

Fine, Kate thought, pulling the quilt more tightly about her. But she knew it would be a long time before either one of them forgot about the drunk on the towpath, and even longer before she stopped worrying about the tunnel.

Chapter Ten

The first thing Kate thought of when she awakened the next day was the tunnel, and she was filled with dread. She gave a start when Seth spoke.

"We'd better have cocoa for breakfast instead of milk," he said. "It's really cold today."

Gray and gloomy, too, Kate thought, glancing out the window. She made her way to the stove, determined not to let Seth see how much she ached, hoping her stiffness would ease as she moved around the cabin. None of the boys they had hired to drive the mules ever complained about being stiff and sore, but of course none of them had ever walked the whole day.

Two men, Kate. *Not a boy my age and a girl.* They never should have attempted it, Kate thought. But it hadn't been "they," had it? She was the one who got them into this, and she had no choice but to go on. To go through the tunnel and then to go on, and on, and on.

After an almost silent breakfast Kate announced, "I'll drive the mules till we get to the mouth of the tunnel, and then you can take over. You can ride Cupid if your feet still hurt."

"I'm not getting on that razor-backed mule of yours again no matter how sore my feet are," Seth declared.

So it wasn't just his feet and legs that hurt, Kate mused as she went to harness the mules. Soon she was walking beside them, every step taking her closer to the tunnel, and her chest began to tighten. With each familiar landmark a reminder that she was drawing near, she had to make a conscious effort not to slow her pace. Her hands grew moist, and she grew light-headed.

There it was. Kate's heart pounded as she saw the sprawling hulk of mountain ahead of her, its rock face broken by the gaping mouth of the tunnel. Her steps faltered, and the team came to a halt without her saying a word.

A boat had stopped just outside the tunnel, and when Seth eased *The Mary Ann* into the bank so it wouldn't drift he asked, "What's the problem with that boat? Do you think it's the drunks?"

"Of course it's not the drunks! Even river scum gets off to an earlier start than we do," Kate snapped. "And there isn't any problem—the captain's just waiting for a light boat to come through, 'cause boats can't pass in the tunnel."

"The light boat's almost out now—I can see the mules," Seth said.

Kate's mouth felt so dry she wasn't sure she could speak, but she managed to say, "I'll light the bow lamp and get us lined up with the portal before I go in the cabin." She ran to light the lamp, then hurried back to the tiller. As *The Mary Ann* moved slowly toward the tunnel, Kate stared at the rudder of the boat ahead of her and tried not to think of anything else. When the boat was properly lined up, she ran into the cabin and threw herself on the bed. Filled with foreboding, she waited for the tunnel to swallow them up.

It was happening. First the shadow of the portal and growing darkness as the boat slid silently into the tunnel, and then murky blackness so thick that Kate could barely see her hand before her face. Her whole body shook as her heart pounded. Why hadn't she remembered to light the lamp in the cabin? Mama had always done that for her. "Oh, Mama," Kate sobbed into her pillow. "If only you were here. I *need* you!"

She tried to remember what Papa used to tell her, tried to remember that boats went through Paw Paw Tunnel every day from late March until early winter. And every single one that entered the tunnel came out safely on the other side. *The Mary Ann* would come out safely, she told herself. But when? If her jaws hadn't been clenched so tightly they ached, Kate would have screamed it out: *When?*

She felt a jolt as the boat scraped along the wooden bumpers that edged the rocky edge of the canal and heard the echo bounce from wall to wall. Kate wondered if Seth was afraid, tried to picture him limping painfully beside the mules, his hand on the wooden railing that edged the towpath ledge. The bow lamp would shine on the boat ahead of him and show the tunnel's low ceiling, but the towpath would be in darkness.

Kate stared into the oppressive blackness that surrounded her and wondered how much longer she could stand it. She felt as though she'd been cowering in the cabin for hours, but she knew it couldn't take more than twenty minutes to get through the tunnel. She began to feel the familiar pressure in her chest, as if she were being crushed by the mass of the mountain above them.

At last the darkness seemed to lift a little, and Kate held her breath, hoping it wasn't her imagination, hoping they were near the downstream portal. Yes! It was slowly growing lighter. She had survived the tunnel again.

Drawing a shaky breath, Kate sat up and tucked in her shirt. Seth's shirt. Her mouth was dry, but there was no time to scoop a dipperful of water from the keg just inside the door. Now she had to steer the The Mary Ann safely out of the tunnel and along the narrow passage where the rock had been blasted away to make room for the canal.

Kate hurried to the tiller deck, and her heart almost stopped when she saw the angled exit of the tunnel just ahead. Leaning all her weight on the tiller, she pushed it as far to the left as it would go. Slowly the bow moved out into the pale daylight, and Kate brought the boat around the treacherous turn between steep rock walls. When she could see the length of the gorge stretching ahead of her, her body went limp with relief.

Seth had left the mules and was limping toward the boat, so Kate wiped her tear-stained cheeks on her sleeve and went to put the plank in place for him. As he came closer, she saw that his face wore the same look of concern it did when he comforted his sister. Kate frowned. If he thought she was a timid little rabbit like Julia, he'd be sure to make another attempt at having a turn as captain. She had to show him that she was still in charge, had to make him think twice before he tried to take over again.

"How are your feet?" she called as he approached.

"They hurt some, but they're better than yesterday," he said, stepping onto the plank. "Are you all—"

"Good," she interrupted. "I hope that means you'll be

able to do your share of the walking soon, 'cause every day you don't, we fall further behind schedule."

"You might at least thank me for driving the mules through the tunnel for you," Seth retorted as he stepped onto the boat.

Looking him straight in the eye Kate said, "You didn't do it for me, you did it because it had to be done. I certainly hope you don't think I've been driving the mules 'for you' the past two days." She turned away to step onto the plank, but not before she saw Seth's face grow pale and his expression harden.

As Kate hurried toward the mules, she told herself that she'd rather be hated for being unreasonable than pitied for her uncontrollable fear of the tunnel. There was only one thing that mattered, and that was getting this boatload of coal to Georgetown so they could turn in their waybill and collect their pay. If anybody's feelings were hurt in the process, that was too bad. Still, she was sorry that she'd had to be mean to Seth after he'd treated her so decently.

Why *did* Seth treat her decently? "For the same reason he didn't go back to Cumberland that first night," Kate whispered. "Because he's trying to live up to what his father told him to do." She felt a growing respect for Seth, and then she was shaken by the thought that her stepfather must be as important to Seth as Papa had been to her. "As important as Papa *is* to me," she said aloud.

The very idea unsettled Kate, and as she walked beside Cupid she became aware of one thing: She didn't want her stepfather to die in the war. Until now, she hadn't allowed herself to think that he might be killed; she had made her mind go blank whenever that possibility crept into her mind. It was one thing to hate a person and something else indeed to wish him dead.

Walking beside the mules, Kate felt a flash of sympathy for her stepbrother. He must miss his father terribly.

Surprised that she no longer thought of Seth as an enemy, Kate decided that if he hadn't been her stepbrother, she might even like him a little. Especially after the matter-of-fact way he'd accepted her fear of the tunnel. Well, here on the waterway Seth wasn't her stepbrother, he was her crew—and Papa always said part of a captain's job was to keep the crew contented. Of course, Papa never had to worry about his crew wanting to be the captain, but that didn't change the truth of what he'd said.

"WHOA, Cupid. WHOA, Junior," Kate said, stopping well before the lock where the boat just ahead of them was rapidly being lowered. She left the mules and walked back to the drifting boat, but Seth gave no sign that he noticed her. He was still angry, and she didn't blame him a bit.

"Hey, Seth," Kate called. "I came back to thank you for driving the mules through the tunnel." When he made no response she turned and walked slowly back to her team, telling herself she didn't care if Seth never spoke to her again. But she knew she did.

Chapter Eleven

That afternoon a damp breeze off the river made Kate shiver. Looking up, she saw that dark clouds were building to the west. An April shower, or a storm? Kate thought longingly of the warmth of the cabin, but she would have settled for being under the canvas awning that sheltered the cabin and the tiller deck.

A chill seemed to settle over her, and Kate frowned. She couldn't very well wear her shawl when she was dressed as a boy, and Seth had only one jacket. "I could wear my oilskin!" she exclaimed. As long as the weather threatened rain, she'd look well prepared instead of foolish. Not that *she* would look either one. Heading back to the boat, Kate called, "Hey, Seth—I need my oilskin."

She watched him disappear into the cabin and quickly reappear to hang the raincoat and hat on the end of the pole and thrust them at her. "Thanks," Kate said, but Seth turned away without a word. How long was he going to stay mad, anyway?

Buttoning the oilskin coat as she went, Kate ran to catch up to the team. Sandy shied as last year's leaves scudded across the towpath just ahead of him, and Kate wished that her faithful Cupid was the lead mule instead. "It's all right, Sandy," she said soothingly, but when she rested a comforting hand on his shoulder, his hide rippled as though to shrug off her touch.

Now the usually mirror-still surface of the canal was wind streaked, and the clouds hung low. Kate caught the scent of rain on the air and muttered, "We're in for a real toad strangler." Other years, rainstorms had seemed an exciting break in the routine, but other years, she'd enjoyed them from the shelter of the awning—or from inside the cabin, if Mama insisted. Guiltily, Kate realized that she'd never once thought of the hired drivers, except perhaps to envy them on the hottest days when she'd have welcomed a cooling shower.

"Hey! Aren't we going to stop and wait out the storm?" Seth shouted, breaking his long silence at last.

Sorely tempted, Kate forced herself to shout back, "We'll never get to Georgetown if we just work when the weather suits us." As captain, she had to set an example. She had to show Seth that boaters keep going no matter what, had to make him forget her early stop the day before.

Five minutes later the rain began. A gentle patter at first, it quickly built into a steady downpour that beat against Kate's oilskin hat so noisily she could barely think. Soon she felt water trickling down the back of her neck, water dripping off her oilskin coat onto her trousers. Seth's trousers. Kate gritted her teeth and walked on as mud began to ooze up between her bare toes. How could she have imagined that driving the mules would be fun?

Kate gave a start when Seth blew the tin horn and

hollered, "HEY, LOCK!" She looked up and saw the blur of the lock just ahead of her. *What if Seth couldn't see far enough ahead to line up the boat?*

She hurried the mules to the downstream gates and was splashing back to catch the snubbing line when she saw something that made her heart pound: The boat was slightly off center. It was too far to the left. Kate raced to catch the coiled rope, dug in her heels, and pulled with all her might—hand over hand, hand over hand, straining until at last she felt *The Mary Ann* move toward her. Above the pounding of the rain she heard Seth's shout and a second later the unmistakable thunk of wood on wood.

Wood on *wood*—not wood on stone. Thank goodness this was one of the locks that had timber cribs to protect the stone walls and guide the boats into the narrow passage! Hearing Seth's shouts, Kate sprinted to the snubbing post to brake the boat.

"What the heck did you do that for? You almost wrecked us!"

Kate stared at Seth. "What do you mean, *I* almost wrecked us? If it weren't for me, you'd have crashed into the crib on the berm side instead of just grazing the one over here!" Angrily, Kate splashed through a puddle to close the upstream gate of the lock. How dare Seth try to blame her for his own mistake!

Back at the snubbing post, Kate waited tensely until she heard the lock tender's call above the sound of the rain.

"Line ready!" she called back. Lowering her voice she said, "Whether you admit it or not, you were way off center, Seth."

"I was lined up *perfectly*. If you hadn't interfered, everything would have been fine. Next time, you mind your own business!"

Kate felt a surge of fury. "Everything about this boat is

my business, Seth Hillerman," she said, her voice shaking. "Everything!" She would have said more, but Seth made a warning gesture, and Kate saw the lock tender trudging toward them through the rain.

"What's the matter with your captain, putting a boy at the tiller in weather like this?" he asked, glowering first at Seth and then at Kate. "Last thing I need is a boat wreck blocking my gates."

"Captain's sick, sir," Kate said, glad the oilskin hat hid most of her face.

Stepping back, the man said, "He's not the one with typhoid, is he? Yesterday we had a report of a captain down with typhoid."

"Our captain's Mrs. Hillerman what used to be Mrs. Betts," Kate said. "She's been feeling poorly lately, but she don't have typhoid, mister."

"Well, you tell her my advice is to lay over before you come to the next lock. Even an experienced steersman would have trouble in weather like this." Without waiting for a response, he sloshed back to the downstream gate.

"I could have told him what's the matter with the captain of this boat," Seth said. "She's as stubborn as those mules she thinks so much of. That's one thing that's the matter with her, anyway."

A gust of wind hit the boat, and Kate was so busy managing the snubbing line that she couldn't answer. It was all she could do to keep *The Mary Ann* from being blown into the lock wall and still give the line enough play while the boat was being lowered to the next level of the canal.

The lock tender was right, Kate thought when she went to push open her side of the downstream gates. They would have to lay over. And Seth was right, too—right about her being stubborn. Still, she wasn't ready to give in yet. Not to the weather, and certainly not to Seth.

But once they were under way again, Kate realized that waiting to lock through had chilled her, and she felt miserable now instead of just uncomfortable. Her feet were so cold she might have been walking through slush instead of mud, and she had to clench her jaw to keep her teeth from chattering. Surely she had made her point by now, hadn't she? Kate had almost decided to stop when the fog began to roll in and Seth hollered, "Tee, yip, YA-ah! Hey, out there—I can't see well enough to steer this thing."

Trying to sound reluctant, Kate called back, "Then I guess we'll have to stop." She fumbled to unhitch the mules, her fingers so numb she could barely make them move, and by the time she had tethered the team and wiped off the harnesses, she was so cold her stomach ached.

Inside the cabin, Kate saw that Seth had built a quick fire and was heating water for tea. "I don't know what you're trying to prove, Kate, but— Hey, you'd better get out of those wet clothes!" he exclaimed when she took off her oilskin. "I'll wait under the awning while you change."

She peeled off Seth's things and shivered her way into her own clothes, but even with her shawl around her, Kate felt cold. She called Seth in, and then she wrapped herself in a blanket and huddled down in the rocking chair.

The kettle began to steam, and Kate groaned inwardly, but before she could force herself up, she saw that Seth was measuring tea leaves into the pot. Hiding her surprise, she told herself, If I can do his work, I guess he can do mine. She watched him pour the tea into two cups and spoon in quite a lot of sugar.

"Thanks," Kate said, reaching out of her blanket cocoon to take the cup he offered. She wrapped her icy hands around it and breathed in the steamy fragrance, wondering if she would ever be warm again. Slowly she sipped the tea and then let Seth fill her cup again.

"What are you thinking about?" he asked as he refilled his own cup.

Kate shrugged and said, "I'm just trying to warm up. What are *you* thinking about?"

"I was wondering how long it's going to take us to get this load of coal to Georgetown," he admitted.

"A lot longer than it ought to, at the rate we're going," Kate said. "It's been three days now, and we're not even a quarter of the way there. We just can't make good time with only one driver. And I didn't mean that as a criticism," she added when anger clouded Seth's face. "It's just the way things are. You can't walk until your feet are healed, and I can't walk any more hours than I have been."

Seth looked down at his feet and said doubtfully, "Maybe by tomorrow I'll be able to do my shift."

"We'll try it like this," Kate said. "I'll do three hours and you'll walk one, and if that works out we'll keep it up all day, and the next day you can do more."

"Sounds all right to me," Seth said. "Once we're both driving, we can make up some of the time we've lost."

It was still going to take them a long time, Kate thought as she sipped her tea. But at least Seth was speaking to her again, and he was no longer accusing her of causing the boat to bump the log crib at the lock.

"You're thinking about something now," Seth said.

"How can you tell?"

"All of a sudden you got a mean look on your face. And I didn't mean that as a criticism," he added. "It's just the way things are."

Kate wasn't sure whether he was mocking her or not. "I was thinking about how the boat hit the log crib," she said, trying not to let a mean tone creep into her voice. "We'd have been in big trouble if it had hit the lock wall instead."

Nodding, Seth said, "It really is hard to see when the rain's coming down like that. It's hard to judge distance."

Was he admitting that it was his fault? Or did he think she'd admitted it was *her* fault? Kate wasn't sure, but she knew that neither of them would bring the matter up again.

"The rain has almost stopped," Seth said, quickly adding, "But it's even foggier than it was."

Good, Kate thought. She still hadn't warmed up, and she didn't think she had the energy to walk another step.

Chapter Twelve

The next day dawned clear and cool, and by the time breakfast was over, Kate barely noticed her stiffness. Her spirits were high as she started out. Not only was it a perfect spring morning, but she knew that after three hours of walking she would have a rest while Seth walked his first hour. "COME up, Cupid! COME up, Junior! Let's make some time here," she urged.

With the canal on her left and the rain-swollen Potomac swirling past on her right, Kate felt as though she were walking on a long, narrow island. She liked it when the towpath was on the riverbank and she could look down at the Potomac flowing below her instead of barely seeing it through the woods. Something in her responded to the untamed river and the relentless, single-minded way it coursed toward the sea.

Kate loved the canal, but the river's power and its unpredictable moods—calm and serene in one place, tumultuous in another—fascinated her. Watching the roiling water always made her feel full of energy and life.

As the waterway followed a hairpin bend of the river, Kate looked ahead at the towpath curving before her and frowned. Something was wrong up there. Squinting into the morning sunlight, she felt her chest constrict—a huge section of the bank had collapsed, and now only a narrow slice of towpath separated the canal from the turbulent river below! If that narrow strip of land gave way, the water in the canal would rush out and sweep *The Mary Ann* down into the river.

Now the Potomac's swirling water looked dangerous instead of exciting, and Kate fought the feeling of panic that swept over her. She moved closer to Cupid and rested a hand on the mule's neck as she forced herself to walk toward the near-break. They had to get across that sliver of path before the whole bank collapsed.

"Tee, yip, YA-ah!" Seth called from the boat, his voice pitched higher than usual.

Looking back, Kate saw that he was shading his eyes with his hand as he stared at the damaged towpath. "Come ashore and give me a boost so I can ride across there on Cupid," she cried, nervously combing the mule's stubby mane with her fingers.

"No! It's not wide enough, Kate—you could be killed," he shouted back.

Killed? The very word rocked Kate with fear. She gasped when a curl of towpath that overhung the water dropped off and disappeared into the canal. While she stood and stared as though hypnotized, a shower of pebbles slid into the water, each one making a perfect circle that rippled outward.

Cupid nuzzled her, breaking the spell, and Kate tore her eyes away from the water lapping at what was left of the bank. "COME up, Cupid," she commanded. "COME up, Junior."

"Stop!" Seth shouted. "Don't risk it, Kate!"

Didn't he understand that she had to risk it? Couldn't he see the danger they were in—danger that increased with every wasted minute? If Seth wouldn't help her, she'd have to hang onto the mule's collar and let Cupid carry her across that way.

Kate walked determinedly toward the narrow strip of land that was all that was left of the towpath ahead of them. But just before they reached it, Cupid planted her feet and refused to budge, and Papa's words echoed inside Kate's head: *Always listen to your mules, my girl. They have an uncanny way of sensing danger, so listen to their warning, even if you don't understand it.*

Kate could understand this warning, though, and she was almost faint with fear. She looked back and saw that Seth had run the boat against the slope of the bank to stop it and was sprinting toward her, a determined look on his face. Too frightened to care if he thought she'd given in to his better judgment, she called, "You're right. It's too dangerous."

"What are we going to do?" Seth asked when he ran up. "The canal's not wide enough for us to turn around."

Trying to keep her voice steady, Kate said, "We'll have to drift past. Go put the fall board in place so we can get these mules on board—and hurry!"

Seth dashed back to *The Mary Ann*, and Kate unhitched Cupid and Junior and ran toward the boat, pulling them along behind her. "Quick—help me get them in the stable," she said, urging the mules onto the ramplike fall board. There was no time to lose.

After they managed to crowd the complaining mules

into the stalls with the other team, Seth asked, "What now?"

"Shove us off the bank, and then give one good push to get the boat moving downstream. I'll steer us past." Unless the bank gave way, and then she'd cling helplessly to the tiller while the water in the canal behind them surged toward the break, carrying the boat down into the river.

Kate's mouth was dry as she watched Seth run for the pole and shove the boat away from the bank, then dig the pole into the mud of the canal bottom and hang his weight on it. Slowly the huge boat began to move, and after a quick look at the near-break, Kate focused her eyes on the water straight ahead of her. But against her will, she felt her gaze drawn to the place where the grassy edge of the towpath had crumbled into the water, only a few inches at first, but then in larger and larger bites. "Oh, Mama, why did I ever leave you?" Kate whispered.

A movement caught her eye, and she saw Seth about to lean on the pole again. "Stop!" she cried. "Didn't you hear me say 'one push?' "

"But we're barely moving! At least let me shove us away from the bank."

"Just do what I say!" Kate's hand shook as she eased the tiller slightly to the left. Far ahead of her, the bow approached the cave-in. It was much larger than she had thought, and the curved rim of towpath that remained looked even narrower than it had a few minutes ago. Kate gasped when a chunk of sod slid into the water and was followed by another shower of pebbles. Scarcely breathing, she stared at the raw earth exposed by the break until the bulk of the boat blocked her view.

It seemed to take forever to drift past the danger area,

and Kate tightened her grip on the tiller and pleaded silently, Just a little farther . . . just a little farther. . . .

At last she could see the ragged edge of the cave-in not ten feet ahead of where she stood, and her scalp prickled. They weren't safe yet—if that bank gave way now, the force of the water rushing out would still catch the boat's stern and sweep them into the river below. Water lapped against the loose earth on the slope beneath the thin strip of packed dirt—all that remained of the towpath—and Kate held her breath as *The Mary Ann* inched by.

At last! Kate felt her body go limp, as if her bones had turned to jelly. She drew a shaky breath and then gulped in another.

"We're past it," Seth said. "Does that mean we're safe?"

"We're safe," Kate said, her voice sounding strange in her own ears. If the bank gave way now, they'd just be left stranded in the mud.

His face still pale, Seth said, "I don't see why you insisted on staying so close to the bank. If I'd been captain, I'd have stayed as far away from that break as I could, and I'd have gone past it a lot faster, too."

"And if you had, that might well have been the end of *The Mary Ann*—and the end of us, too." Kate's voice shook with emotion. "The farther you are from shore and the faster you go, the more damage there is from your wake. So if you'd been captain just now, that bank might have given way, and if it had, the water rushing out would have carried *The Mary Ann* through the breach and smashed us to pieces down in the river."

In her mind's eye, Kate saw *The Mary Ann* swept stern first into the Potomac as the water rushed through the break in the canal, saw the boat splinter when it hit the rocks in the river below, saw a lifeless mule float—

"Hey, are you all right?"

Blinking away the horrible image, Kate gave a jerky nod. But she wasn't all right. She needed to throw herself into Mama's arms and sob out what she had seen, needed to be hushed and petted and told that everything was fine.

"Listen, maybe you'd better go lie down or something, Kate. You look—"

He was doing it again—treating her like he did Julia. "Stop it!" Kate cried. "Don't talk to me like that!" Then, embarrassed by her outburst, she said, "Listen, Seth, I know you're trying to help, but I can't decide what to do next if you keep talking to me."

"Do next?"

"We aren't the only ones on this waterway, you know." Kate paused for a moment to let that sink in, and when Seth's face grew even paler she said, "This is what we should do. We're almost to the next lock, so the quickest way to keep traffic off this level is for you to get down there as fast as you can and have somebody ride back along the road to warn the lock tender upstream."

She looked at Seth's bare feet and asked pointedly, "Do you want to run all the way, or are you going to ride that razor-backed mule of mine?"

"I guess I'd better ride Cupid," Seth said, following Kate to the stable.

"You go ahead. I'll hitch up General and Sandy and start down there to meet you," Kate said as they put the mule fall board in place. She was surprised at how easy it was for the two of them to manage it.

By the time Seth was on his way and the team was ready to start, Kate felt almost herself again. Now if only they could get to the next lock before the water level dropped and they were left high and dry. They didn't need another delay.

As soon as she was back on the boat, Kate called for

the mules to start, and then she dashed to the cabin. She peeled off Seth's clothes and grabbed her petticoat and dress. Struggling into them, she buttoned the dress, snatched her bonnet from its peg, and ran out of the cabin.

Leaning on the tiller to steer away from the bank, Kate called for the mules to "come up" as she tied her bonnet under her chin. She hoped she looked presentable in spite of her haste, because the lock tender's wife was a friendly woman who loved to talk with the boaters. But even more, Kate hoped that Seth's warning would come in time to keep other boats off the level. The fog that had stopped *The Mary Ann* the afternoon before would have delayed traffic all along the waterway, so maybe—

Someone shouted her name, and Kate saw Seth riding a sleek black horse along the road on the berm side of the canal. She watched him thunder past, leaning low over the horse's neck. She hadn't known he could ride like that! Turning her attention back to the mules, Kate called, "COME up, there, Sandy! COME up, General." Had they slowed their pace without a driver, or did they just seem slow in comparison to Seth's breakneck speed?

Kate looked down the towpath and saw men on horseback rapidly approaching. She thought it was a cavalry patrol until the riders came closer and she saw that they were carrying picks and shovels. She recognized the lock tender and two of his sons, and when the men passed her, she saw that the others—on muleback—were the four brothers who crewed *The Rosemary*.

As she neared the lock, Kate saw the lock tender's wife standing by the snubbing post, beckoning her on, and she waved. *The Mary Ann* moved into the lock, and Kate tossed the woman the snubbing line. "Thanks for the help, Mrs. Connally," she said.

"When we sent your driver off to warn the folks up-stream he said you'd need a hand," the woman said. "But you know, I could have sworn he said his brother was at the tiller."

Seth hadn't known she was going to change into her own clothes! Thinking quickly, Kate said, "Maybe he told you he was *my* brother. He's my stepbrother, really—Mama married his father last fall."

Mrs. Connally clapped her hands. "That's wonderful, Katie! Run inside and tell her I've got the kettle on the stove, just waiting to make us a nice pot of tea."

Wishing with all her heart that Mama really was inside the cabin, Kate said, "She can't visit today, ma'am, 'cause she's feeling poorly." Quickly changing the subject, she gestured to the boat tied up below the lock and said, "I see that Seth got here in time to keep *The Rosemary* from locking through.

"She'd just pulled into the lock when he rode up, but we hauled her out and filled the chamber up for you."

Glad that she'd been able to distract Mrs. Connally from her questions about Mama, Kate said, "I saw that her crew was part of your husband's work party." She noticed that while they were chatting, the youngest Connally son, a strange, silent youth, had closed both upstream gates and now stood patiently beside the downstream gates. "I think Zeke's waiting for us," Kate said.

Mrs. Connally turned to him and called, "Line ready!"

Kate waved to Zeke, and he lifted a hand in greeting before he began cranking open the paddles at the base of the gate. Above the sound of rushing water, Mrs. Connally asked, "When did your mama take poorly, Katie?" But Kate kept her eyes on Zeke and pretended she hadn't heard. How was she going to keep the woman from finding out that Mama wasn't on board?

The stone walls of the lock chamber seemed to rise around Kate as the boat was lowered to the next level, and then the huge wooden gates ahead of her slowly began to part. Looking up, she could see that Mrs. Connally was leaning all her weight against the heavy beam of one gate while her son opened the other almost effortlessly.

Kate called to the mules, and as *The Mary Ann* moved slowly out of the lock, Mrs. Connally said, "You can tie up wherever you like to wait for your stepbrother, Katie."

Kate took the boat as far downstream as she dared before she stopped the mules and steered the boat toward the berm, but to her dismay, this didn't discourage Mrs. Connally. "Put out your plank, Katie," she called.

"I—I can't let you come aboard. Mama's too sick for visitors."

"Then I'll write a note and send Zeke for the doctor, right away," the woman said, her voice showing her concern.

"No! Please don't do that!" Kate cried, adding lamely, "She's not *that* sick."

Mrs. Connally put her hands on her hips and said, "Set out that plank, Kate Betts, and be quick about it. I'll be the judge of how sick your mama is."

Miserable, Kate put the plank in place, and head bowed, she waited for the woman to come aboard.

"There, now, Katie. I'm sure your mama will be fit as a fiddle in no time at all," she said when she saw the girl struggling for control.

"Mama isn't here," Kate choked out. "She's back home in Cumberland 'cause the doctor said she has to stay in bed till her baby's born. And it's taking Seth and me *forever* to get this load of coal to Georgetown."

"Well, I guess it is!" Mrs. Connally exclaimed. "Two

youngsters trying to manage all by themselves? I can't imagine why your mama ever allowed—"

"Mama doesn't know we've gone," Kate interrupted, accepting a handkerchief. "She does now, of course, but—"

Mrs. Connally put her arm around Kate and said, "You come on over to the house and tell me all about it, dear. We'll put our heads together and figure something out."

"But the mules—"

Calling to Zeke, Mrs. Connally said, "See to Katie's team, won't you, son?" And then she led Kate to the lock house where she gave her a cup of tea and listened to her story until the lock tender came in, shaking his head angrily.

"Rebel sympathizers, that's who done it," he said. "One of them traitors with a pound of black powder took advantage of that fog and blowed it up in the night."

"You mean somebody did that on purpose? Even though people could be killed if a boat was washed into the river?" Kate asked, aghast.

"This is wartime, Katie, and folks get killed in wars."

Kate stared at him. She had never thought about people who weren't soldiers getting killed. She didn't even think very much about soldiers getting killed, since all the ones she'd seen had seemed more like guards than fighting men. And the letters from Seth's father had been filled with talk about drills and roll calls rather than battles.

"When young Paul Revere gets back, have him ride the mare downstream to the carpenter shop and ask 'em to send their work scow up here," Mr. Connally said, turning to his wife. Before she could answer, a horn blew and he said, "I'd better get out there and let 'em know what's going on. If any more light boats come along, send their crews up to help us. Have Zeke set out some more tools." He left the room, grumbling about Rebel sympathizers.

It wasn't long before Zeke came into the house, and Mrs. Connally gave him his father's message. The boy bobbed his head in a quick nod but didn't answer, and when he had gone his mother said quietly, "Zeke's afflicted, you know. He hasn't spoke a word in his life. Understands pretty much anything you tell him, though, and he can do the work of a man."

Kate didn't know what to say, so she just stared down at her teacup, wishing that Mrs. Connally hadn't brought up Zeke's affliction. Shouldn't that be one of the things "people don't talk about"?

But Mrs. Connally hadn't finished. "Sometimes you think he has the mind of a child, and sometimes he seems—" she searched for the word—"well, almost wise. But he's always good. You know, Katie," the woman mused, "if I had a favorite of all my boys, it would be Zeke, because he's kind. He doesn't have a mean bone in his body."

Mrs. Connally leaned forward to fill their cups again. "Now, finish your story, Katie. Start with how you cut off all your beautiful hair."

Chapter Thirteen

It was past noon by the time Seth returned from delivering the lock tender's message to the carpenter shop. Mrs. Connally called him to come to the house, and when he saw Kate he stopped short and stared at her. "Your hair!" he exclaimed. "It's— I like it."

Kate patted the ringlets that covered her head, and Mrs. Connally said, "I done a right nice job, didn't I? Pair of scissors and a curling iron is all it took, and now our Katie won't be ashamed to take off her bonnet. Looks like a girl again instead of a scrub brush, don't she?"

Seth nodded his agreement. "Now her mother won't be quite so shocked to see her when we get back."

"Speaking of your mother," Mrs. Connally said, frowning as she turned to Kate, "it's high time you let her know the two of you are all right. Jot down a message for her, and I'll send it along with the first boating family headed upstream. The Kellys got an early start this year, so they ought to be passing here soon," she went on, thinking aloud. "I'll bet Lenore would be happy to deliver a note if I gave her a bit of fudge or some gingerbread. She knows where you live, doesn't she?"

"Yes, but if Lenore takes Mama a message, pretty soon everybody will know she's not on *The Mary Ann*," Kate objected, "and then we won't be able to say I'm in the cabin taking care of my mother if somebody asks for me when I'm driving the mules."

Glaring at Kate, Seth said, "Address the note to Mrs. Steller, then. She'll take it over to your mother."

Kate could feel her stepbrother's unspoken rebuke, could almost hear him accusing her of not loving Mama. What was the matter with her? Why couldn't she have been the one to think of a plan? And why hadn't she thought of sending a message in the first place?

Miserable, Kate took the paper and pencil Mrs. Connally found for her and began to write.

Dear Mama,
Please don't worry about Seth and me. We are fine, and so are the mules. I hope you are feeling well. I miss you a lot and wish you were here on the waterway with me.

Kate read over what she had written and knew she should have said "with *us*," but instead of changing it, she signed the note "Your loving daughter, Katie" and began to address the envelope. After she wrote their neighbor's name she hesitated a moment, and then added under it, "Next door to the yellow house where Captain Betts lived."

"There, that's done," Mrs. Connally said as she took the envelope and propped it on the windowsill. "Now come have a bite to eat before you go on your way. And don't you worry," she assured them, "because even though I don't

99

approve of what you've done, I know you mean well, and I'll keep your secret for your mother's sake. And," she added mysteriously, "I've figured out a way to make the rest of your trip a bit easier. While you're eating, I'll tell you about it."

The fried chicken Mrs. Connally had sent with them was a welcome change from bean soup, Kate thought at suppertime. But the woman's insistence that they take Zeke along was what Mama would have called a godsend. Kate saw that Seth was watching the tall, stoop-shouldered boy who sat placidly between them at the small table. Why, Seth looked like he wished Zeke weren't there, Kate noticed in surprise. Well, he *was* there, and she was glad of it. They'd make much better time with a third person on the crew.

"Zeke's good with the mules," Mrs. Connelly had assured her, "and he'll do whatever you say and never give you a bit of trouble." That would certainly be a welcome change from Seth.

"More milk, Zeke?" Kate asked, and when the boy nodded, she filled his glass. "You can drive the mules in the dark, can't you, Zeke?" He nodded again. "Do you mind working the last shift every day?" He shook his head, and Kate turned to Seth.

"Instead of six-hour shifts, I think we should change drivers each time we lock through—unless the locks are really close together. That way, we won't get so tired, and steering won't be as tedious. You'll be able to walk some tomorrow, won't you?"

Seth gave a perfunctory nod, and Kate almost had to bite her tongue to keep from asking if he, too, were mute. She turned to Zeke again and said, "I put fresh hay on the bunk in the hay house, and the blankets your mama sent with you are out there, too." Zeke nodded, and a moment later he pushed back his chair and left the cabin.

"What's the matter with you, anyway?" Kate asked Seth.

Seth shrugged. "I don't know how to act around somebody like him. Somebody who sits like a lump and never says a word."

Surprised, Kate said, "Just act the same as you always do." *Treat him as if he were just the same as anyone else, Katie,* Papa had told her, *but don't make the mistake of forgetting that he isn't. He needs our respect, but he needs our protection, too— especially protection from people who would make sport of him because he's different.*

"You don't act the same toward Zeke," Seth objected. "You're a lot nicer to him than you are to anybody else."

"I'm just trying to make him feel at home, Seth."

"That's more than you ever did for Julia and me back in Cumberland."

Kate stood up and began to clear the table. "Zeke can't look out for himself, and the two of you can." At least Seth could.

"It sounds like you're saying I should be pleased that you aren't nicer to me."

Kate poured hot water from the kettle over the dishes, and in the blank tone of voice she used when she was angry but trying not to show it, she said, "You should be pleased that I trust you to steer *The Mary Ann.*"

" 'Trust' me to steer? You wouldn't *let* me steer if it didn't suit your purposes."

Kate turned to him and said flatly, "You wouldn't be on this trip at all if it didn't suit my purposes, Seth Hillerman. But it suits your purposes, too, don't forget, assuming that you want to get through next winter. You and Julia and that baby."

Seth's eyes darkened with anger, but he spoke quietly.

"That baby will be just as much your brother or sister as mine, don't forget."

"I wish I could forget!" Kate cried, her eyes filling with tears. "I wish things could be like they were before Papa died, when it was just Mama, Papa, and me."

"At least you can remember your father," Seth said, sounding sad now instead of angry. "I barely remember my mother."

Wiping her eyes, Kate asked, "How long ago did she die?"

"When Julia was born."

Kate's hands flew to her face. "She died having a baby? What if that happens to *my* mother?"

Blushing a little, Seth said stiffly, "I doubt that your mother will die in childbirth, Kate, but if she did, I think you would feel very sorry for the way you've treated her lately."

For a moment, Kate stared at Seth, and then she burst into tears. Sobbing, she buried her face in her arms. She was sorry *now!* If only—

A melody seemed to tumble into the small cabin, and Kate raised her head to see Zeke leaning against the door, playing a harmonica. She recognized the tune of a hymn her mother loved, and hiding her face again, she cried even harder, wishing Zeke would play something else.

Almost as if he had read her mind, he began to play a ballad, and as Kate listened, the flow of tears gradually stopped. By the time Zeke put away his harmonica, she had resolved to be a better daughter, to try to please Mama, and to help her the way she always had before Mama married Seth's father. Before she'd turned herself into Seth and Julia's mother, too.

Seth turned away from the window where he'd been staring into the darkness and said, "Thanks for playing for us, Zeke. You're really good." The older boy nodded and slipped out of the cabin.

"See?" Kate said shakily. "You did it. You treated him just like anybody else."

Chapter Fourteen

"Hey, what's all that?" Seth asked two days later, pointing ahead to a series of structures lining the canal berm.

"It's a cement mill," Kate said. "They mine limestone out of the mountain, bake it in those kilns on the hillside there, and grind it into a powder."

Eyeing a huge pile of coal, Seth said, "Say, maybe we could sell our cargo here."

"Our waybill says Georgetown. Besides, wouldn't you rather carry coal for steamships fighting the Rebels instead of bringing it here to fuel those limekilns on the hillside? I'd think you'd rather help save the Union than help make concrete."

Ignoring Kate's lecture, Seth craned his neck to see the tall chimneys belching smoke. "Just look at those smokestacks!" he exclaimed.

Kate wrinkled her nose in disgust. How could Seth be so impressed by an ugly place like this? It was noisy and dirty, too—even the air was dirty here, and a layer of pale dust covered everything in sight. Keeping the boat close to the bank, Kate was about to steer past a line of boats waiting to be loaded with barrels of cement when she sensed that *The Mary Ann* had slowed. Glancing down the towpath, she saw that Zeke had stopped to stare at the mill's giant waterwheel.

Kate raised her voice so she could be heard above the thumping of the wheel and the rumble of machinery. "Keep those mules moving, Zeke," she hollered. Always obedient, he hurried the team along, but it was obvious that he hated to leave the busy scene along the canal.

As the boat eased by the loading dock, Kate said, "We're almost to Hancock, and we'll stop there to buy us each a straw hat. It's too warm for this cap of yours."

"Besides, a hat will shade your face and keep—"

"And keep me from getting more freckles," Kate interrupted, determined to rob him of the satisfaction of saying so.

Seth looked at her in exasperation. "I was going to say 'keep the sun out of your eyes,' but you're right—it *will* keep you from getting more freckles."

Kate felt her face grow warm and knew that it was turning red. But she also knew she'd brought her embarrassment on herself. She was glad when Seth broke the uncomfortable silence.

"Are you going to change into your dress when we go to town?"

"It would be easier to buy a straw hat if I'm dressed like a boy, don't you think?"

Seth nodded. "Maybe so," he agreed reluctantly, "but up close, you still don't look much like one."

An hour later, after they had tied up at Hancock, Kate went to Zeke and said, "Seth and I are going to the store to buy straw hats like yours. Do you think you could wash the outside of the cabin while we're gone?" Kate had worried that Zeke would insist on going with them, but to her relief, he nodded and went to find a bucket.

Seth followed Kate when she went into the cabin to count out some coins from the sugar bowl, and to her surprise he pointed to the scuttle and said, "Rub some coal dust on one arm, and a bit on your cheek, too. So you'll look more like a boy," he explained. "That's a little better," he said when she had done it and turned to him for approval. "Now pull your shirt tail out—just on one side, not all the way around," he said, sounding exasperated. "And you'd better wear my cap, even though it's pretty warm, to cover up those ringlets Mrs. Connally gave you."

Tucking her thumbs behind the straps of the suspenders Mrs. Connally had provided, Kate raised her chin and said, "How's this? Do I look tough?"

Seth snorted. "You look pretty silly, if you ask me."

Well, I *did* ask him, Kate told herself, smarting at his reply. "Here, you'd better take the money," she said. "If you do all the talking, maybe no one will pay attention to me."

They went ashore and walked between two warehouses to reach the street. "There sure are a lot of taverns," Seth said. "Where's the store?"

"We have to go to the next street and turn right," Kate said. She followed him up the hill, putting her hands in her pockets and trying to match her walk to his, until he turned and said, "I see it—halfway down the block."

A stagecoach rumbled by, passing a delivery wagon just as they reached the general store, and Seth turned to watch the high-stepping horses. Comparing them to the mules, Kate thought as the stage disappeared around the corner, leaving a haze of dust in its wake.

Inside, Seth led the way past barrels of flour and sacks of sugar, past kitchen utensils and tools and kegs of nails, to the back of the store where bolts of cloth and ready-made clothing were displayed. "There they are," he said, pointing at the hats. "And stop looking at those ribbons," he hissed.

"I wasn't," Kate hissed back.

"And what can I do for you fellows today?" the store-keeper asked, walking toward them.

"You can sell us each a straw hat, sir."

The man looked them over and whipped a tape measure from his pocket. "Let's see what size you'll be wanting," he said. After the storekeeper wrapped the tape around Seth's head, Kate took off her cap and stood while he measured hers. "A lot of girls would like to have curls like yours, sonny," he said, and after checking the sizes of several hats, he chose two and motioned Seth and Kate to the front of the store.

"Be with you in just a moment, Hal," the storekeeper said as a man came into the store, and still holding the hats, he rang up the cost on his cash register and told them the total.

"Aren't you going to let us try them on?" Kate asked, unable to keep still any longer. "What if they don't fit?"

Without looking at her, the man said, "They'll fit. Now do you want them or not?"

Seth counted out the money, and after it was safely in the cash drawer, the man handed them the hats and said, "I hope you understand that once you boys have had your grubby hands on these you can't return them."

"And *I* hope *you* understand that we won't be doing business at your store in the future," Seth said.

"We'll make sure that none of our friends do, either," Kate threatened as they left.

The sound of men's laughter followed them down the sidewalk. "We'll shop in the stores along the canal, where our business is appreciated," Kate said, seething. "Grubby hands, indeed."

"Well, I guess we do look pretty grubby, especially compared to somebody like that man over there," Seth said.

Kate turned to see a well-dressed older man who had just stepped out of the hotel across the street. "And whose idea was it for me to rub coal dust all over myself?" she asked.

"Well, you have to admit he didn't catch on that you're a girl, in spite of your curly hair."

Kate tipped the wide brim of her hat so it kept the sun out of her eyes and said, "Well, first thing I'm going to do when we get back to the boat is *wash*." She was glad Mama hadn't heard what that storekeeper said.

Chapter Fifteen

Kate sighted across the tip of the flagpole and steered *The Mary Ann* into the lock. Ahead of her, Seth stood poised to wrap the line around the snubbing post, and Zeke waited at the stable door, ready to hurry Cupid and Junior off the boat for their shift.

Safely inside the lock, Kate relaxed her grip on the tiller and watched Zeke unload the fresh mules and then snap his fingers to urge the other two up into their stable while Seth managed the snubbing line. It certainly was easier with a crew of three. Seth seemed to have gotten used to having Zeke around, and it was obvious that he was glad he no longer had to help care for the mules or their gear. And, of course, they were making better time now.

Kate listened to the gurgle of the water running through the openings at the base of the wooden gates ahead of the boat, and she felt the peculiar sensation of sinking below the stone walls of the lock as the water level dropped. Then the lock tender and Seth, on opposite sides of the canal, rested their weight on the long beams that extended from the lock gates and slowly pushed them open.

They were on their way again, passing a light boat that was waiting to lock through. It looked like *Forever Mine*, but Kate didn't recognize either the captain or the driver. Why would Captain Fielding rent out the boat he'd grown up on? The boat his family lived on year-round? Deciding that there probably weren't two boats with purple trim, Kate called to the other captain and asked, "Aren't the Fieldings going to be on the waterway this season?"

The other captain shook his head. "Not this waterway, anyhow. The captain's gone and joined the navy, and his wife's so mad she rented out his boat. She and the young-uns are living with her sister now." He laughed and shook his head.

By the end of the week, everybody up and down the canal will have heard that story, Kate thought, vowing to make sure no one other than Mrs. Connally found out that "Nate the mule driver" was really Kate Betts.

"Play me a tune, Zeke," Kate said when the older boy joined her on the tiller deck. Zeke whipped his harmonica out of his pocket, and his music, sometimes rollicking, sometimes plaintive, held Kate's attention until he stopped in the middle of a song. Kate saw Zeke shade his eyes with his hand and stare ahead to where the canal seemed to end at a strangely angled lock.

"It's all right, Zeke," Kate said. "We're coming to Little Slackwater, where the boats go out into the river for a while and the towpath's on a rock ledge on the shore."

Zeke's eyebrows rose, and he tapped the edge of the boat and pointed to the river.

"That's right," Kate said, preoccupied with positioning

the boat to enter the lock. "The boat goes through that channel ahead of us and then into the river." She gave a start when Zeke stamped his foot, and when he had her attention, he shook his head determinedly and pointed from himself to the river. "Don't worry, Zeke—it's perfectly safe," Kate reassured him. Well, safe enough, anyway.

The bow of the boat was slipping between the lock walls now, and Seth was waiting for Zeke to throw him the snubbing line. But to Kate's surprise, instead of tossing the line to Seth, Zeke jumped off the boat with it and wrapped it around the post himself. Then, with a series of gestures, he made it clear that he was taking Seth's place as mule driver.

"What's the matter with him, anyway?" Seth asked as he joined Kate on the tiller deck.

"Apparently he didn't like the idea of being aboard while we're on the river," Kate said. She tried to sound nonchalant, but her hands felt clammy at the thought of steering on the slack water for the first time. She reminded herself that the lock tender didn't allow boats into the river when the water was dangerously high.

Seth's eyes widened. "You never told me we'd have to take the boat in the river!" he exclaimed.

Raising her voice above the sound of the water rushing from the lock, Kate said, "You can walk with Zeke, if you want to. If you're scared." The boat moved rapidly lower, and she half wished that *she* could walk instead of steering. If only Papa were here beside her!

"I didn't say I was scared," Seth said stiffly. "I just don't understand why we have to go on the Potomac."

"See how the mountain comes right to the edge of the river here?" Kate asked. "Well, since there wasn't any room to build the canal, they just blasted away enough rock to make the towpath and let the boats go on the river for the next half mile or so," Kate explained. "The mules will cross over on that bridge," she added, pointing.

The lock gates opened, and Kate watched Zeke snap his fingers and lead the mules across to the berm side. The click of hooves on the stone ledge stopped, and the team leaned forward, stretching the towline taut, then stepped and leaned again until the boat began to move.

Watching Seth, Kate could see that although he seemed determined to act unconcerned, he was becoming more and more nervous as the boat approached the river. She hoped he couldn't tell that she was nervous, too.

The minute *The Mary Ann* was on the Potomac, Kate sensed a difference, felt it move with greater ease. She pushed hard on the tiller, keeping the boat away from the rock wall of the towpath ledge, then swung the tiller in the opposite direction to keep from going too far out into the river. The towline, which had always looked so long, suddenly seemed short. Kate's blood ran cold at the thought that the mules—and Zeke—would be dragged into the river if she let the boat drift too far away from them.

But now she had oversteered and was heading for the rock wall again! Kate pushed the tiller, leaned her weight on it when the boat didn't respond, and then gasped when the delayed response was more than she'd intended.

Beside her, Seth hollered, "Hey, Zeke! Make those mules move faster. Get them going fast enough that the towline's stretched tight!"

Kate wrestled with the tiller, sure that the boat was out of control, until she felt a subtle difference, felt the boat respond and then hold its course. Weak with relief, she saw that the mules were almost trotting and that the towline was taut. "What made you tell him to speed up the mules?" Kate asked, wondering how her stepbrother could possibly have known something she didn't know about boating.

"I remembered how sometimes you have to run with a kite to keep it flying the way you want it to, and I thought it might work for boats. Hey, what's that noise?" Seth asked, suddenly alert. "It sounds like a waterfall up ahead."

"That's water flowing over the dam that backs up the river so we can navigate here."

Seth didn't answer, and Kate saw that he was looking ahead to the dam, where the river dropped from sight. "How often does a boat go over that, anyway?" he asked, his voice tense.

"Over what? The dam?" Kate made her voice sound surprised as she pointed *The Mary Ann* toward the river lock that would take them back into the canal. "You don't have to be afraid of that."

Seth said shortly, "You don't have to be afraid of the tunnel, either."

Kate was too busy leaning on the tiller, fighting the current as she steered toward the inlet lock, to answer him. At last *The Mary Ann* nosed into the narrow passage, and Kate was able to relax. She hoped Seth thought she hadn't heard him over the roaring water, hoped he hadn't noticed how hard it had been for her to turn the boat. She didn't remember it being hard for Mama, but then last year they weren't on the river when it was swollen by spring rains.

While Zeke snubbed the line, Kate asked the lock tender, "Does your wife have any bread for sale today, Mr. Elliot?"

"Do I know you, boy?" the man said, frowning at Kate.

She'd forgotten she was wearing Seth's clothes! "Sorry, sir," she said. "I'm Nate, and this is my brother, Seth."

"We've never been down the waterway before," Seth added, "but a fellow tied up next to us last night said we could buy good bread at Elliot's Lock."

"Usually you can, but the missus didn't bake today," Mr. Elliot said. "Funny," he added, looking from Kate to Seth and then back to Kate again, "I know I've never laid eyes on your brother before, but I'm beginning to think I must have seen you someplace."

Kate was speechless, but Seth distracted the lock tender by pointing to the opposite shore and saying, "Looks like there was a bad fire across the river, sir."

"Federal troops burned the mill over there, sonny," the man said. "A band of Rebels had holed up in there while they was trying to blow up the dam so boats couldn't navigate the slack water. We wouldn't of been able to divert river water to fill the canal below here, either. Anyway, I guess the Federals burned the mill to make sure them Rebs wouldn't have no shelter if they tried that again."

"They tried to blow up the dam? When was that?" Seth asked in alarm.

"Winter before last. There was a lot of action around here for a couple of days, the Rebels trying to destroy the dam and the Feds shooting at 'em. Anyhow, them Rebs finally did manage to blow a hole in the dam—had to wade out in the water to do it. Didn't take us long to patch it up again, though." Mr. Elliot sounded smug.

Kate saw the concerned look begin to leave Seth's face when he saw the Union troops that guarded the dam now. She was sure he'd been wondering what would have happened if the Rebels managed to blow it up while *The Mary Ann* was in the slack water.

When they were on their way again, Seth said, "Aqueducts, the tunnel, slack water—what other interesting

114

things do I have to look forward to on this trip?" Kate launched into a recital of all the locks and levels from there to Georgetown, and when she finished, Seth marveled, "How do you remember all that, anyway?"

"I've been going up and down this waterway my whole life, don't forget," Kate said, not mentioning that during the past winter she'd made the trip countless times in her imagination, as well. Made it with Papa. She looked across the wide expanse of placid water to the fields where a man was plowing. "Aren't you glad you don't have to walk back and forth behind a plow hour after hour?" she asked, changing the subject.

"It would be pretty dull to walk all day and still be at the same place when night came," Seth agreed.

Kate wondered if he liked watching the scenery change along the towpath as much as she did, if he liked seeing the long stretches of woods or farmland broken occasionally by a town or village. Seth could have his New York and Philadelphia and all those other places he'd visited, Kate thought. She'd rather be on the waterway.

"Hey, what are we coming to now?" Seth asked, peering ahead as he steered the boat out of an aqueduct that afternoon.

"Williamsport," Kate said. "There's a big warehouse at the loading basin just ahead." As they passed the wharf, men were rolling barrels of cement down the fall board of one boat while a boom swung a huge iron bucket filled with coal from the hatches of another.

Kate almost wished their waybill was for Williamsport. After a week on the canal, they still weren't even halfway to Georgetown. The McLains, who had left just ahead of them, were probably already there. Well, with a crew of three they were making better time now, Kate reminded herself. Turning to Seth, she said, "We'll pass the halfway point later today."

"It sure is taking a long time to get there," he said.

Hearing him put her thoughts into words made Kate feel even more discouraged, but she said, "We're going a lot faster now that we have Zeke. And now that you can do your fair share," she added pointedly.

"That's right, rub it in," Seth said, his voice hard. "Blame me for something I couldn't help."

He could have helped it if he'd walked barefoot that first day, Kate thought, but for once, she didn't feel like arguing.

"All finished?" Kate asked when Zeke came back from polishing the bow lamp the next afternoon. He nodded, and she said, "You've done a good job of cleaning up the boat. Are you going to get some extra sleep now or keep me company while I steer?"

Zeke's answer was to pull out his harmonica, and as Kate listened, she wondered how he had learned so many tunes. Now he was playing "Home, Sweet Home," Papa's favorite, and it brought a rush of memories that filled her eyes with tears. The music stopped abruptly, and Kate glanced up to see Zeke staring at her, a horrified expression on his face.

"That was my papa's favorite song," she explained as she wiped her eyes. "He died December before last. The doctor said it was pneumonia." Kate glanced at Zeke and saw that he was listening attentively. "I—I still miss him a lot," she went on, "especially when I'm boating. He taught me everything I know about the canal, 'cause he didn't have any sons to teach it to."

Zeke frowned and pointed down the towpath toward Seth.

"He's my *step*brother," Kate explained. "My mother married Seth's father, and less than a year after Papa died, too. Mama said she and Papa had promised to love each other 'till death us do part, and since death had parted them she needed somebody else to love. Somebody who was there."

Zeke nodded his head, and since he still seemed interested, Kate kept talking. "But now Seth's father isn't there either, because he went off to fight in the war. Poor Mama. And on top of everything else, I've been so mean to her lately—"

Kate broke off and raised the horn to her lips. She blew three blasts and then yelled, "HE-EY, LOCK!" She grinned when Zeke put his hands over his ears. "Papa always said that with my voice, we hardly needed a horn."

Chapter Sixteen

"Another aqueduct!" Seth exclaimed. "What river does this one take us over?"

"It crosses a creek, not a river," Kate said as she lined up the boat to enter the aqueduct. "It's Antietam Creek."

Seth stared at Kate. "Antietam Creek? The one that ran red with blood after the battle last September?" he asked, his voice hushed.

"Well, it's near where the battle was," Kate said, "but I don't know whether—"

"You never bothered to tell me your precious waterway went right through the middle of the war, Kate."

"That battle was last year, and we aren't 'in the middle of the war,' anyway."

"We might as well be. Every time I turn around, I see an army camp or a picket post."

"Yes, but those are Union soldiers, don't forget. We haven't seen a single Rebel."

"Maybe not, but we've seen the damage they've done. I've counted at least a dozen mills or bridges they've burned, and—"

"None of that has anything to do with us, Seth."

He went on as if she hadn't spoken. "—they tried to destroy that dam at the end of Little Slackwater, too. And just last week they tried to blow up the canal, don't forget."

"That was Rebel sympathizers, not the army," Kate reminded him.

"Well, it's still the war, isn't it? And it certainly had something to do with us."

Seth was right, Kate thought uneasily. As the boat moved out of the aqueduct she said, "Well, I'm sorry you're afraid, Seth, but I don't think there's anything to worry about."

"I'm not worried, and I'm certainly not afraid," Seth said shortly. "I just think you should have told me. And I can't believe you weren't even going to point out where Antietam was."

For a moment, Kate was confused, but then she realized he meant the battle, not the village that stretched along the creek banks. She hadn't known Seth was so interested in battles.

As *The Mary Ann* neared Harpers Ferry that afternoon, Kate wrinkled her nose at the smell of coal smoke that rose from the factories in the small industrial town. Turning to Seth, she pointed across the Potomac to the opposite shore where the United States flag flew over an army camp that seemed to cover every field and hilltop.

"When the war first started, the Rebels were camped over there," she said, "and they tried their best to wreck the canal—they broke some of the lock gates and did a lot of other damage. We got in just one trip before the government closed down the canal for two whole months. And then last year Mama and I only got in a few trips because of the war. I *hate* those Rebels." Silently, she began the familiar litany again: If they hadn't stopped traffic on the canal, Mama wouldn't have been in Cumberland all those weeks last season and she wouldn't have met—

"Is that they only reason you hate the Rebels? Because of what they did to the canal?"

That, and what they did to my life, Kate thought. "Isn't that reason enough?" she asked.

Seth's voice rose in exasperation. "You know what's wrong with you? You don't see any farther than the end of your own nose. It doesn't matter to you that the country has split in two and a lot of men are going to die before the South is brought back into the Union again. No, all you care about is that the Rebels messed up your precious canal."

"You needn't act so high and mighty, Seth Hillerman, 'cause for all your talk, I'll bet all *you* really care about in this war is what happens to your father."

Seth opened his mouth to protest, then seemed to think better of it. His shoulders slumped and he said, "It's been an awfully long time since he's written to us."

Hearing the misery in his voice, Kate wished she could take back her angry words. "Mama has probably heard from him by now," she said, embarrassed that she hadn't even been aware that her stepfather's frequent letters had stopped coming. Maybe Seth was right—maybe she really didn't see any farther than the end of her nose. "I'm sure Mama's had a letter from him," she repeated.

"Or maybe one from the government saying he's been killed."

"They send telegrams," Kate said, leaning on the tiller,

"and she'd have had one before we left if that was why he hadn't written. There's some other reason. You'll see." There *had* to be some other reason—she'd wanted her stepfather to disappear, not to die! Kate felt a tightness in her chest. Don't be silly, she told herself sternly. Hate couldn't kill a person any more than love could keep somebody alive.

She waved to a little boy sitting on the sagging steps of one of the small houses that lined the road along the berm side the canal, then eased *The Mary Ann* past a boat tied up in front of a store. Kate frowned, trying to think of reasons why her stepfather's letters might have stopped. Surely he'd have written if he could have. He wouldn't want Mama to worry, especially now that she was going to have a baby.

"You're thinking about the baby, aren't you?"

Startled, Kate turned to Seth and asked, "How did you know that?"

" 'Cause you were scowling. Most girls like babies. How come you don't?"

"I'm not like most girls. Haven't you figured that out yet?"

Seth met Kate's eyes and said, "I guess you think you're better than most girls. I know you think you're better than Julia."

The truth of his words hit Kate with a jolt. "Being different doesn't have to mean better—or worse, either," she said evenly. *Always be yourself, Katie.* That was what Papa had told her. *Be yourself, but be your best self.*

She was certainly being the best captain she could be, but was she being her best self? Making a special effort, Kate said, "Listen, Seth, I'm sure your father's fine. His letter might have gotten lost, you know."

121

"It might have," Seth said, but he didn't sound convinced.

Kate saw him swallow hard, and she thought, It was terrible when Papa was sick, but at least we were with him. We didn't have to wonder how he was, and when he died, we knew it right away. It was terrible, but at least we knew.

Later, as Seth walked beside General and Sandy, Kate looked ahead at the narrow V the Potomac had cut through the mountains. The canal and towpath hugged the river, squeezed in between the shore on the right and the railroad on the left. An eagle soared over the river, and Kate was so intent on watching it bank and glide that she wasn't consciously aware of the sound of an approaching train until its engine was in sight.

Clouds of gray belched from the smokestack and hung thinly in the air above a long line of boxcars, and Kate scowled. Trains might be fast, but they were noisy and smelly, too.

The engine was almost opposite Seth when the engineer blew the whistle. The shrill blast frightened Sandy, and he reared, jerking General's harness and pulling him back so that he nearly knocked Seth off his feet.

"Grab the bridle! Grab Sandy's bridle!" Kate shouted from the boat. But Seth seemed reluctant to approach the frightened animal, and while he hesitated, Sandy twisted in the harness and his shoulder struck Seth, knocking him to the ground.

All Kate could think of now was the mule's iron-shod hooves, and she watched helplessly until Seth rolled out of the way. The train whistle blasted a second time, its mocking sound tearing through the air, and Sandy stamped and brayed. Kate breathed a sigh of relief when she saw Seth scramble to his feet.

"That's just one of the reasons boaters hate the B & O," she fumed as she brought the drifting boat close to the bank beside Seth and the mule team. "That railroad's been trying to put the canal out of business for years. At the beginning of the war all the boaters cheered when we heard how the Rebels had burned the railroad bridges and torn up the tracks. It was a lot better for us when the trains weren't running."

"Maybe so, but it was a lot worse for the country when there weren't any trains to carry soldiers and supplies for all those months," Seth retorted. "You wouldn't care about that, though. You don't care about anything but boating." Without giving Kate a chance to respond, he turned to the mules and called, "COME up," and they set off again.

Kate stared after him, taken aback by the exasperation in his voice. She steered automatically as she brooded on what her stepbrother had said. "Boating is all I have left to care about," she whispered, "and even that isn't like it used to be."

Life on the waterway used to be a long, leisurely holiday, Kate thought. Other years, she'd steered *The Mary Ann* for the pleasure of it, helped care for the mules because she loved them. But now she did those things—and so many others!—because they had to be done.

Was that why she had loved boating so much all those other years? Because it seemed like play instead of work? Puzzled, Kate frowned. Papa had loved boating, and it hadn't been play for him. He had liked working outdoors and being his own boss, Kate remembered. And Mama? Mama would be happy anywhere, as long as she was with her family.

Maybe that was why *she* had loved boating so, Kate

thought. Maybe it was just being with Mama and Papa, and then being with Mama and remembering Papa. Maybe it was the long, lazy days and cozy evenings together, the three of them at first and then just herself and Mama. Now, though—

Suddenly, Kate was aware of the clack of wheels in the distance, and her hand on the tiller tensed. She saw Seth drop back to walk beside Sandy, but as the train rounded the curve, the engineer, riding with his elbow out the window of his cab, simply lifted a hand in greeting as he passed.

Seth waved back and turned to watch as several flatcars filled with soldiers clattered by. Kate watched, too, wondering what it must be like to sit on one of those swaying platforms as the train snaked its way through the mountains. If it was going to Cumberland, it would be there in no time at all. Frowning, Kate thought of the days that had passed since *The Mary Ann* left the boat basin at the edge of the city. After all this time, they were still more than sixty miles from Georgetown.

"I don't care if trains are faster," she said, "I'm never going to ride on one." It would take more than a friendly engineer to change her opinion of the B & O.

"*Now* what!" Kate exclaimed when Seth stopped the mules and headed toward the boat. Sometimes she wondered if they would ever get to Georgetown.

"Hey, Kate! I think Sandy hurt himself when he reared back there. You want to come take a look?"

By the time she had steered the boat into the bank, Zeke had the plank in place. Kate followed him to shore, but he reached the mules well ahead of her and was kneeling beside Sandy when she ran up. "Let's see," Kate demanded.

Seth stepped aside and said, "It's a cut a little bit above his left hind hoof."

Kate winced at the sight of the dust-caked wound, but Zeke stood up and tapped his chest, then pointed first to the boat and then to Sandy. Kate wasn't sure exactly what he meant, but she knew he was taking charge, and she was grateful.

"Do you think he knows what to do?" Seth asked as they watched Zeke lope back to the boat.

"His mother said he was good with mules."

"I sure hope Sandy doesn't kick him," Seth said.

Kate didn't answer. None of their mules had kicked anyone, but that didn't mean they never would—and of all the mules, Sandy was the least predictable.

When Zeke returned, he handed the scissors and some clean rags to Seth and put down the bucket of water and the can of kerosene he was carrying. But before he set to work, Zeke looked into Sandy's eyes for a long time and then trailed his hand along the mule's side and down its leg to just above the cut.

Kate held the halter firmly with one hand while she stroked Sandy's neck with the other. In soothing tones she said, "Zeke's going to take care of you, Sandy. He's going to make your leg as good as new." She watched Zeke gently clean the wound and then pour kerosene over it, watched him take the scissors from Seth and begin to clip away the hair around the cut.

After Zeke had bandaged the mule's leg Kate said, "I guess we'd better switch teams even though it isn't nearly time yet." And that meant they would have to stop early so they wouldn't overwork Cupid and Junior. Oh, well, Kate thought glumly. They were already so far behind schedule that one more delay scarcely mattered.

Chapter Seventeen

"Hey, look at the blockhouse over on that island!" Seth exclaimed, pointing.

"There's one a mile or so farther along, in the middle of the island, too," Kate said, easing the boat a little to the left. "The army built them after the battle. That's Harrison's Island," she added as an afterthought.

Seth's brow puckered into a frown and he said, "I never heard about any battle on Harrison's Island."

"Well, you heard about the Battle of Ball's Bluff, didn't you? The bluff's across the river in Virginia, but our soldiers got there from the island, and that's where they brought the wounded afterward."

"I've heard of the Battle of Ball's Bluff, all right," Seth said bitterly. "The Rebels really trounced us. Do you still claim that the canal isn't in the middle of the war, Kate?"

"That was a year and a half ago," she reminded him. "They fought the battle just a couple days before we passed here on our way home. Papa heard all about it—and about the upside-down canal boat—when he was buying groceries at Edward's Ferry."

Kate paused, and Seth prompted, "So what did he hear?"

"Well, some of the soldiers from the army camp at the ferry were in the store, and they told Papa how our men had crossed from the island to the Virginia shore and followed a path up to the top of the bluff, where there's a big clearing. That's where the fighting was later on. After all our men finally got up there, the Rebels ran out of the woods and charged right at them. Pushed some of them over the edge."

"So where does the upside-down canal boat fit into the story?" Seth asked.

"I'm coming to that. Some Union general had his men haul a light boat out of the canal, take off the hatch covers, and drag it over to the river. They used it to take men from Harrison's Island to the foot of the bluff before the battle, and later they used it to ferry the wounded back to the island," Kate told him. "But then a whole lot of soldiers who managed to run back down the cow path piled on, too, and practically sank it. The Rebels on the bluff kept firing at them, and when a couple of the men poling the boat across were hit, they slumped over the race plank and unbalanced the boat enough that it flopped over."

"Capsized," Seth said.

Kate nodded. "They used other canal boats to move the wounded down the waterway to the army hospital at Edward's Ferry," she added, glad she hadn't seen those boatloads of suffering men.

That trip had been her last one with Papa. "I'm not going to risk my family's safety, and I'm not going to risk having the army confiscate my boat." That was what he'd said after he came back from the store and told the terrible story he'd heard from the soldiers. So they had finished the season before the end of October, with weeks of good weather still ahead of them.

But her last trip down the waterway with Mama had come even earlier the past autumn—late summer, really—when word came that the whole of General Lee's Rebel army was headed north toward Maryland and would soon reach the Potomac fords. Kate sighed. She had hated having to end the season early for the second year in a row, but Mama hadn't minded at all. Mama had been glad to be home in Cumberland so she could see Seth's father again. So she could marry him.

A subtle change in the boat's movement brought Kate back to the present. She peered ahead and saw that Zeke had stopped the mules and was kneeling beside Cupid's right foreleg.

"Is she hurt?" Kate called, immediately thinking of the small cut near Sandy's hoof. Zeke shook his head, and she tried again. "Has she lost a shoe?" Zeke nodded, and thinking aloud, Kate said, "We just changed teams, so we can't replace her with one of the other mules. I guess we'll have to stop for the night."

She turned to Seth and said, "You unload General and Sandy while I heat the soup." Even though tying up early now and stopping at the blacksmith shop tomorrow would delay them, Kate was glad to have an excuse to spend the evening inside the cabin. She didn't think she'd ever get used to the way the warmth of a spring afternoon could turn to bone-chilling cold once the sun went down.

In the middle of the night, Kate woke with a start. Wide awake, she lay in bed, her body rigid, convinced that something was wrong but not sure what it was. And then she heard it—an eerie sound that rose to a crescendo and then slowly faded away. It sounded like a gate creaking, except that it was much too loud, and there were no gates here.

Kate strained her ears and listened to the silence for what seemed like hours until she heard the sound again. What *was* it? And where did it come from? She was about to wake Seth when she saw him tiptoe from his mattress to the window and pull back the curtain. "Are the mules all right?" she whispered.

"They're fine—I think they're sleeping."

"What do you think that noise is?"

"I don't know," Seth answered. "Shh! I think somebody's on the boat."

On the boat! Kate was telling herself he had to be mistaken when the door to the cabin burst open, and in the instant before it slammed shut again, a looming shape filled the moonlit rectangle. Kate felt like she was being suffocated by a wave of fear. And then in the terrible silence that filled the cabin, she sensed that it was Zeke.

"It's all right, Zeke," Kate said when she could speak again, and she got up to lead him to his chair at the table. "Did you see something that scared you?" He shook his head and Kate asked, "Was it that noise?" Zeke nodded vigorously. "Well, a noise can't hurt us," Kate said, trying to keep her voice steady.

Though she couldn't see Zeke's face in the darkness, his cowering posture showed his terror, and her own fear returned. If only she could bury her head in Mama's lap and concentrate on Mama's hand stroking her hair, Mama's calm voice saying that everything would be all right. If only Papa were here to keep her safe!

"I'm sure there's a good explanation for that noise," Seth

said as he joined them at the table. "Tomorrow we'll probably laugh at how scared we were."

"I hope so," Kate said, "but meanwhile, how do we get
through the night?"

"Zeke can play for us," Seth said.

"Yes, play for us," Kate echoed. That would take their
minds off the terrible sound—or at least keep them from
hearing it. "I'll light the lamp."

Zeke pulled his harmonica out of his pocket and began
to play. At first, the notes wavered, as though he didn't
have quite enough breath, but then he seemed to lose
himself in the music. When he began a hymn, Seth sang
along with him, his voice clear and pure.

Kate's eyes widened. She hadn't known Seth could sing!
Music must run in his family, she decided, remembering
how his father had led the singing class at church. To her
surprise, she found that she had thought of the man without the usual rush of anger, and she realized this wasn't
the first time that had happened. Maybe it was because
she'd started thinking of him as Seth's father instead of as
her stepfather—or Mama's husband.

As she listened to the boys' music, Kate felt the tension
begin to drain out of her body, and by the time they
stopped, she was no longer afraid. "That made me feel a
lot better," she said.

"I guess we should try to get some sleep now," Seth
said. He saw Zeke frown and added, "You can bring your
blankets in here if you want to."

But Zeke shook his head and moved his chair so that
it was smack in front of the door. He folded his arms
across his chest and sat there looking solemn and brave.

Seth started to blow out the lamp, but Kate said, "Maybe
we should just turn it down low. So Zeke won't have to

sit in the dark," she added quickly. Zeke nodded energetically, and Seth seemed more than willing to agree.

Back in bed at last, Kate was sure she would never fall asleep, and she could hear Seth turning restlessly on his mattress across the cabin. Long after his even breathing told her he was sleeping, Kate lay in the silence and listened for the creaking sound. She knew she hadn't imagined it, since it had waked the others, too. . . .

The sun was high by the time Kate heard Seth stirring the fire in the small iron stove the next morning. Her eyes were heavy as she stumbled out of bed, and it seemed to take her forever to fix breakfast. Seth appeared to be his usual self, but Zeke sat nodding over his oatmeal.

"Go to bed, Zeke," Kate said. "Since you kept watch all night, you needn't work this morning. We'll manage without you." They'd manage, but it would mean an even later start, Kate thought. This trip was just one delay after another.

It was Seth's turn to drive the mules, and while he was harnessing General and Sandy, Kate changed into her dress and checked to make sure that the braids she'd sewed onto her bonnet hung naturally. She was looking forward to a quick visit with the lock tender's daughter when she heard it again—the same creaking sound that had waked them all the night before. But in the daylight, it didn't seem nearly so frightening.

Kate peered out the cabin window and saw that Seth was standing on the towpath, looking into the woods by the canal. Curious, she slipped out to the tiller deck to see what he found so interesting.

"I've solved our mystery," Seth said. "Look up there."

Kate looked where he was pointing, but she saw nothing unusual in the treetops. She was about to ask Seth what on earth he was talking about when the bare trees swayed a little in the light wind at the same time she heard the creaking sound again.

"There!" Seth said. "See how the trunk of that dead tree leans across the maple next to it? When the wind blows they rub together. Didn't I tell you that there had to be some good explanation for that noise?"

Kate nodded, wondering how something so ordinary could have frightened them all so, how a *tree* could have cost them hours of sleep and made them get such a late start. "I'm ready when you are," she said, taking her place at the tiller, and Seth called for the team to "come up."

When they reached the village at Edward's Ferry, Kate steered the boat into the basin above the lock and unloaded Cupid from the stable so Seth could take her to the blacksmith shop. Handing Seth one of the coins from the small hoard she kept in the sugar bowl, Kate said, "While you're having Cupid shod, I'm going to buy groceries, and then I'll be at the lock house visiting my friend Amy."

She had just walked into the store when a cheerful voice said, "Well, Katie! We were wondering why we hadn't seen *The Mary Ann* yet this season. Hold that door for me, won't you dear? Tell your mama I'd stop and visit with her if Mr. Green didn't have it in mind to make up the time we lost by stopping early last night so we wouldn't have to pass that island in the dark."

Kate stared after her mother's friend as the woman hurried toward *The Princess*, which was tied up in the basin, and then she turned to the storekeeper. "Was that Harrison's Island she was talking about, Mr. Morgan?" Kate asked. When he nodded, she mused, "I wonder why they didn't want to pass it in the dark."

Mr. Morgan lowered his voice and said, "That's near where the battle was, you know."

"I know, but what's that got to do with it?"

The man shrugged and looked away. "All I can say is, anybody that's tied up along there since then says they'll not do it again. They claim that all night long you can hear the ghosts of all those poor dead soldier boys."

Before Kate could tell him about the tree trunks rubbing together, the door opened and a group of officers from the army camp at the ferry came in. The storekeeper gave them a hearty greeting and said, "I'll be with you as soon as I've helped this pretty young lady."

Kate blushed and said, "All I need is a wedge of cheese, two pounds of soup beans, and a pound of oatmeal."

"How about some cocoa to take the chill off these cool evenings?" the storekeeper suggested, setting a box on his counter.

Tempted, Kate hesitated a moment before she shook her head. Their cocoa was almost gone, but they still had plenty of tea.

"Give the lass the cocoa," one of the soldiers said, putting a coin on the counter. He waved her protests aside and said, "I have a daughter your age back home, lass. Haven't seen her since the war began."

"I'm sure she misses you even more than you miss her," Kate said. "And thank you ever so much for the cocoa."

She paid for her purchases and headed for the door, wondering if Seth would say she was wrong to let the officer pay for the cocoa. "I just won't mention it," she whispered as she walked toward the lock house. She wouldn't mention that people thought the place they'd tied up last night was haunted, either. She wasn't going to say the words "dead" and "soldiers" in the same sentence. Not while Seth was so worried about his father.

Chapter Eighteen

Kate looked up at Seth as she played out the line around the snubbing post the next day. "Hear that roaring sound? That's Great Falls," she said.

"Will we be able to see the falls?" Seth asked, his voice eager.

"No, but you'll see the Potomac gorge, and that's pretty exciting. After we've gotten through this group of locks, you'll have a good view."

She had the best view, though, Kate thought an hour later as she looked down on the frothing water that thundered past more than sixty feet below the towpath. She looked back at the boat to see Seth's reaction, but he was staring at the earthworks Union troops had dug on the hillside that rose from the berm.

Kate turned her attention back to the raging Potomac a giddying distance below her. She was sorry when the towpath swung away from the river and she could no longer see the rushing torrent.

Soon the canal began to widen into a small lake, and Kate murmured, "Widewater, already." She began to think ahead, visualizing what would come next—first, seven closely spaced locks, then two more at greater intervals, and finally, just before the Georgetown locks, the coal yard. All the locks in this stretch of the canal made it slow going, but at least there wasn't a boat just in front of them to delay them even more.

She'd switch places with Zeke at the first of the Seven Locks, and Seth could take over from him at the lock just beyond Little Falls, Kate decided. It was better when they walked five or six miles at a time rather than five or six hours.

It didn't seem long before she saw a stone marker ahead of her, and even though it was too far away to read, she knew that "10 MILES TO W.C." was carved into it. She felt a stir of excitement. Only ten miles to Washington City, and about half a mile less to Georgetown, where their coal would be unloaded.

"I knew we could do it, Cupid," Kate exulted, proud that before the day was over, they would have brought *The Mary Ann* the whole length of the waterway. With their slow start and all the delays, it had taken them almost two weeks to make the trip, but they had done it.

The way home should go faster, Kate thought, but even so, it would take them longer than other boats with a crew of three because their work days were shorter. How did other boaters manage to wake up before dawn? And how did they manage to stay awake at the tiller in the cold darkness?

Absently, Kate noticed that the spicebush growing along the towpath was about to bloom, its blossoms still tight little knots of yellow. She broke off a twig and chewed on the end of it, enjoying the cinnamon-like flavor before she spit out the woody fibers.

This trip has been a walk into spring, Kate thought, raising her eyes on the budding trees that gave the woods a faint haze of pale green. She walked on, so intent on looking for the patch of trout lilies that bloomed along this stretch of towpath each April that she was startled when Seth blew the horn. It was time to change shifts already!

Much later, Kate turned to Zeke and said, "You know, I'm a little scared about coming into Georgetown. Last year, Mama and I stayed on the boat the whole time we were in port, 'cause she said a city waterfront wasn't a decent place for women and girls. I guess I'll dress like a boy while we're there, just to be on the safe side."

Kate lapsed into silence, thinking how satisfying it was to talk to Zeke. She could tell him anything. It was different with Seth—he could answer back.

"Do you like Seth?" Kate asked impulsively. Zeke nodded, and Kate said, "I do too. For a long time I didn't, but I do now." It was easier to like him here on the waterway.

Kate lapsed into silence, and Zeke took his harmonica from his pocket and began to play. Suddenly he stopped in the middle of a song and stared downstream at a bridge high above the canal and river. Covered wagons pulled by mule teams were crossing the span, and Kate said, "Those are army wagons. The government has a lot of soldiers protecting Washington City." Sunlight glinted off the barrels of guns that showed through the cannon ports of the fort on the heights above, and a shiver went down Kate's spine.

An hour later, Zeke pointed excitedly to a spire reaching up from among the buildings clustered along the bluff above the canal.

"That's one of the churches in Georgetown," Kate said. Georgetown! Her feelings a mixture of relief and triumph, she whispered, "We made it, Papa." She looked ahead to where the river side of the canal was lined with warehouses and the towpath ran along the berm side at the base of factories and mills. Pointing to the bridge that took the towpath to the other side of the canal, Kate said, "Once Seth takes the team over that, we have less than half a mile to go."

But Zeke's eyes were on the long, wooden bridge that crossed the river. "Before the war, that was an aqueduct to carry boats over to the Alexandria Canal in Virginia," Kate told him. She had always wondered what it would be like to cross high above the Potomac here where it was so wide.

As they approached the coal yard, Kate saw that a boat was being unloaded and one other boat was waiting ahead of them. Not too long a delay this time, then. "Tee, yip, YA-ah!" she called, and as she eased *The Mary Ann* toward the bank she said, "Zeke, I need you to unload Cupid and Junior so that Seth and I can take the teams to the Canal Company stable while we're in port."

Kate watched Zeke head for the stable, and she thought how nice it was to be obeyed without question. Why couldn't her stepbrother simply accept that she was the one in charge?

When Zeke came back on board, Kate said, "Seth and I are going take the mules to the stable, now. While we're gone, I want you to stay in the cabin, or in the hay house if you'd rather, but keep out of sight." The boy frowned, and Kate explained, "It's for your own good. I don't want anybody to pick on you because you're different. Because you don't talk."

For a moment, Zeke stared at the floor, but then he

gave a slow nod, and Kate was sure she had never seen anyone look so sad. "If you want to wait for us in the cabin, you can finish up that gingerbread I bought yesterday," she said. A smile lit Zeke's face, and as he hurried inside Kate thought, It doesn't take much to please him.

Even though she was dressed as a boy, Kate felt uneasy as she and Seth led the mules along. She couldn't forget that Mama wouldn't even let her off the boat when they were in Georgetown the year before.

"Come *on*, Seth," she said when her stepbrother stopped to watch a crane swing a huge bucket of coal from a canal boat to a horse-drawn railroad car. As his eyes moved along the spur of track that led to a ship anchored at the wharf, Kate said, "You'll have plenty of time to watch when they unload *The Mary Ann* tomorrow."

Kate could see the crowded waterfront that stretched ahead of them with lumberyards and brickyards and warehouses on the river side of the canal, tenements and mills and small businesses lining the towpath side. Hastily built shacks were squeezed in wherever there was even the smallest space, and people—almost all of them men—were everywhere.

It hadn't been like this when she was here with Papa two summers ago, Kate thought, her eyes on the rough-looking crowd loitering in front of one of the tenements. There were soldiers everywhere—pickets at the ferry landing, off-duty troops going in and out of the stores and taverns along the towpath—but they were such rowdy, rough-looking men that their presence didn't make Kate feel any safer. She was glad it wasn't far to the stable.

After they left the teams and started back to the boat, Kate felt even more apprehensive. As she and Seth threaded their way through the crowds on the towpath, she began to silently repeat the poem Mama liked so well. *One step and then another . . .*

They came within sight of *The Mary Ann*, and Kate was horrified to see smoke curling from the open windows of the cabin. "Fire!" she cried, breaking into a run. She was breathless by the time she followed Seth up the plank and onto the boat. They burst into the cabin to find smoke pouring from the coal stove—and Zeke huddled in the far corner.

Coughing, Kate led him outside while Seth fought his way through the smoke to the stove and opened the damper.

A woman Kate didn't recognize came out onto the tiller deck of the boat tied up next to theirs and called, "You need any help over there?"

"Thanks, but we can manage," Kate called back, her eyes smarting. "It's not a fire—the cabin's just full of smoke 'cause the damper on the stove was shut."

The woman looked dubiously at the gasping Zeke and said, "That boy must not be right in the head, staying in there instead of getting away from that smoke."

"Why *didn't* he get out of the cabin?" Seth asked, joining Kate as Zeke stumbled away.

"Because I'd said for him to stay inside. Now help me air the place out. Swing the door back and forth to fan some fresh air into the cabin."

Kate turned away, trying not to think about what might have happened if she and Seth hadn't come back when they did. What if someone had tried to rescue Zeke and he'd fought them off? Worse yet, what if no one had come and Zeke had *died?* Kate shuddered, seeing for the first time that his unquestioning obedience could be dangerous. If Zeke had died, it would have been her fault!

Quickly putting that thought out of her mind, Kate

called to Zeke, who sat leaning against the hay house with his face buried in his hands. "It was a good idea to start the fire so I could cook supper. Next time, just make sure the damper's open so the smoke goes up the stovepipe instead of into the cabin."

Zeke looked up, frowning, so Kate added, "That little handle on the stovepipe points up when the smoke can go up. That's how I remember it."

"If I'd done something that stupid, you wouldn't be so nice about it," Seth said, appearing beside her. "I've got the smoke out," he added.

"Already?" Kate asked, ignoring his first comment. She went into the cabin and saw that though the air no longer hung heavy with smoke, a hazy film clung to the window glass, and the small living quarters had an acrid smell. But more fanning wouldn't help that.

Kate gathered up the blankets so she could take them outside to air. Too bad it wasn't summer, so they could sleep on the flat roof of the cabin tonight. Wistfully, she thought of the muggy August nights when Papa would say, "Well, my girls, this looks like a night to sleep out under the stars." Last year, she and Mama had slept outside on one of the hottest nights, but it hadn't been the same at all.

Kate's arms were so full of blankets she could hardly get through the door. "Help me spread these out," she said when she saw Seth sitting idly, watching a ship steam away from a loading dock on the river. "I'll go ahead and fix supper soon as that's done." Raising her voice, she hollered, "Hey, Zeke!" When he poked his head out of the hay house, Kate called, "I need you to put some more corncobs in the stove and stir up the fire so I can heat the soup."

Zeke clumped across the hatch covers toward the cabin

with a bucket of cobs, carefully avoiding the blankets Kate and Seth were spreading out to air. Watching him, Seth said, "In a minute I'll go in and make sure he does it right this time."

But Kate said impatiently, "Leave him be—he's not going to make that mistake again. What's the matter with you, anyway?"

Seth's answer was to give his end of the last blanket a hard yank, but Kate had half expected that and quickly let go. She watched Seth stumble back a few steps, fighting to keep his balance. Kate could hardly believe that just that afternoon she'd told Zeke she liked Seth. What had gotten into him all of a sudden?

Chapter Nineteen

After the coal had been unloaded late the next morning and *The Mary Ann* was tied up in the boat basin, Kate turned to Zeke and said, "Remember, now, I want you stay in the cabin while we're gone. We won't be long."

With Seth walking beside her, Kate headed for the Canal Company office to hand in their waybill and collect payment for the coal they'd delivered. She turned to Seth and said, "Let me do the talking—don't even say a word unless I ask you something."

A few minutes later Kate forced herself to walk past an unsavory-looking sailor lounging near the door as she led the way into the Canal Company building. Nervously, she slid the waybill through the space below the bars of the cashier window. The clerk looked at it, then leaned forward and frowned at her.

"Where's your captain, boy?" he asked.

"She don't want to leave the boat—says Georgetown's

no place for ladies," Kate said, adding, "Me and my brother are crew for her."

The man shook his head and counted out some bills, then stamped the waybill and wrote something on it. He put it all in an envelope and handed it to Kate, saying, "Now you boys take that straight to your captain, and don't get any ideas."

"Me and my brother are honest lads, sir," Kate said, an injured look on her face as she stuffed the envelope in her pocket. She could hardly wait to give Mama all that money.

After they left the building, Kate had the uneasy feeling that someone was watching her, and when she looked back, she saw that the sailor she'd noticed on their way in no longer lounged near the doorway. He was following them.

Kate's mouth was suddenly so dry she wasn't sure she could speak, but somehow she managed to croak, "L-look behind us."

Seth glanced over his shoulder, then grabbed Kate's hand and began to run. They raced down the street and around the corner, headed for the Canal Company stable. They ducked inside, and at the first empty stall, Seth gasped, "In here, quick!" But when Kate pulled away, he followed her to Cupid's stall.

The big mule nuzzled first Kate and then Seth when they huddled in the straw beside her. Kate felt sick in her stomach when she heard a bleary voice mutter, "If they're in here, I'll find 'em. I'll find the two of 'em, I will."

Kate clung to Cupid's foreleg and willed the sailor not to find them. She couldn't bear the thought of returning to Cumberland empty-handed, the thought of having nothing to show for their long trip down the waterway.

"You! Get out of here, you hear me?"

A stable hand! They were saved.

"I don't mean no harm," the bleary voice whined. "I'm just lookin' for our two cabin boys, 'cause our ship's about ready to cast off."

"You heard me," the stable hand said. "You get out, and don't come 'round here again, or I'll holler for the law the minute I lay eyes on you."

When the stable hand began to whistle and Kate heard water splash into buckets in the stalls closest to the door, she drew a deep breath. She was about to stand up when Seth whispered, "Not yet—that man might be waiting for us."

By now, Kate was feeling cramped, but the possibility of the sailor lurking outside the stable made that seem unimportant. She was wondering how much longer they should stay hidden when Seth sneezed.

Moments later, they were being dragged out of the stall. "Well, I'll be— It's those cabin boys! That runt of a sailor was telling me the truth."

"No, he wasn't," Seth began, "he—"

"He was after us! Trying to steal our money!"

The stable hand glowered at them. "And where would a couple of cabin boys get money? Come along with me. The least I can do is try to find that sailor and—"

"You don't understand!" Kate cried. "We—" But she was interrupted by a surprised grunt as the man doubled over in pain. Before she was sure what had happened, Seth was pulling her out of the stable.

Squinting in the sunlight, Kate said, "This way," and she led him uphill, away from the canal.

"Where are we going?" Seth asked, glancing over his shoulder.

"To the post office so we can mail the money home to

Mama." Kate was rewarded by the look of respect on Seth's face. "Come on, it's not far."

A few minutes later, Kate was addressing the envelope while Seth kept an eye on the door. On the back of the waybill she scribbled, "We're fine, and we're starting home tomorrow. I hope you are feeling well. Your loving daughter, Katie." She folded the money into the waybill and sealed it all into the envelope. After she mailed it Kate said, "I've still got two of the pennies I brought to buy sweets, and there's a store right across the street."

They were poring over the glass jars of candy on the counter when a voice behind them cried, "There you are! I thought I'd find you here." Before either of them could react, the sailor grabbed Kate's arm and dragged her behind him as he propelled Seth toward the shop door, firmly grasping the back of his shirt collar. Turning to the storekeeper, he said obsequiously, "Beggin' your pardon, sir, but we're about to cast off, an' we need our cabin boys."

"Let go of me!" Kate cried, struggling to pull away. Looking back at the surprised storekeeper she called, "Get a policeman, mister—we've never seen this man before in our lives."

The sailor gave her arm a jerk and said, "Quite a sense of humor this one has."

Outside, Kate caught hold of a lamppost and yelled, "Help! Somebody help—" Her cries ended in a gasp as the sailor gave her other arm a cruel twist.

"You try that again, an' I'll tear off yer arm an' beat you over the head with the bloody end of it," he snarled, and he yanked her away from the lamppost with such force that Kate almost believed him. Frantically, she looked for Seth, and her heart sank when she saw that he was gone. How could he leave her like this?

No one on the crowded street seemed to think anything amiss about a sailor dragging a protesting boy along behind him. And no one noticed when the sailor pushed Kate into a narrow alley and held her against him while he reached into her pocket. Kate sank her teeth into the man's arm, and he howled with pain as he flung her against the wall. "You'll give me that envelope, if you know what's good for you, boy," he snarled.

Kate gulped when she felt the point of a knife blade pressed against her neck. "I don't have it," she gasped. "Honest! We mailed it." The man swore, and Kate said, "I'll show you." She pulled both her pockets inside out, and the pennies she'd planned to spend on candy hit the ground and rolled away.

"Gave that money to your brother, that's what you done!"

"We saw you following us, so we ran to the post office and mailed it home to our mother," Kate said.

The sailor's face twisted with such anger that Kate feared for her life, and he snarled, "Why, you little—"

"There he is! Stop him!"

At the sound of Seth's voice, the man bolted down the alley, but half a dozen boatmen pounded after him. Kate's knees felt so weak she had to lean against the wall, but when she saw the concerned look on Seth's face she pulled herself together and said, "Let's get out of here—come on!"

They wasted no time getting back to *The Mary Ann*. Safe on the boat, they sank down onto the hatch covers, panting, and Seth asked, "Did that man hurt you?"

Kate rubbed her sore arm. "Not much, but it's a good thing you came when you did." She wondered how she could have imagined that he'd abandoned her.

"I ran into a tavern and yelled that a man was trying to

make off with my sister, and a whole table full of boaters jumped up."

"They must have wondered what had happened to her," Kate said, tucking in her shirttail. For a moment, Seth looked puzzled, and Kate wondered if she would have to remind him that she was dressed as a boy, but then he laughed.

This was the first time she'd ever heard Seth laugh, Kate thought as the contagious sound brought a smile to her face. But the smile faded as she realized why she'd never heard him laugh before, as she remembered her relentless campaign to make everyone regret the marriage she hadn't been able to prevent.

"Hey, all of a sudden you don't look so good. What's wrong?"

"Nothing," Kate said shortly. "I'm going inside."

After a late lunch of bread and cheese, Seth said cheerfully, "If we aren't starting home till tomorrow, I'm going to have a look at Washington City."

"You can do that on some trip when we have to wait in line to be unloaded," Kate said. "This afternoon we have to scrub down the boat and get rid of all this coal dust." She ran her finger down the wall by the table, making a clean track in the thin layer of grime. "We have to gather up the coal left along the sides of the hatches when *The Mary Ann* was unloaded, too."

"Why this sudden urge to clean down there when you've never even bothered to keep the cabin neat?"

Kate's eyes narrowed, but she managed to control the flare of anger that threatened to burst forth. "It's not a 'sudden urge.' It's what boaters always do. Any coal that's left after *The Mary Ann*'s unloaded belongs to us—it's what keeps us warm all winter. I want you and Zeke to shovel the lumps into sacks we can sling across the mules when we get home. And that's an order from your captain, by the way," Kate added.

"That order doesn't have anything to do with running the boat, so I don't have to obey it. Zeke can clean out the hatches by himself."

Kate was tired of arguing. "Then I'll help Zeke while you scrub the cabin inside and out."

But before Seth could reply, Zeke pointed at Kate and shook his head adamantly, then tapped his chest and nodded.

"Well, if you think you can manage by yourself, I'll help Seth scrub. You know where to find the sacks and a shovel."

After Zeke left the cabin, Kate said, "I didn't realize you were more concerned about staying clean than getting the job done, Seth."

"The job's getting done, isn't it? As long as Zeke's along, you and I don't have to do the dirty work. And don't look so shocked, Kate. We both know who cleans *The Mary Ann* and mucks out the stable."

"That's because Zeke doesn't steer," Kate said indignantly. "The two of us drive the mules and steer, and he drives the mules and does the chores. It's perfectly fair."

"Zeke could steer—between the locks, anyway—and you know it. But you like things the way they are."

"Are you suggesting I'm not treating Zeke fairly?" How dare Seth talk to her like that!

"If the shoe fits, wear it. But if you don't stop arguing and start scrubbing, you won't be finished by dark."

Kate glared at Seth. If he hadn't come to her rescue barely an hour ago, she'd have a few words for him. "Come on then," she said. "Let's get started."

"You can start whenever you like. I already told you I'm going to see Washington City."

Speechless, Kate stared after her stepbrother as he sauntered out of the cabin. How dare he! Who did he think he was, going off to see the city when there was all this work to be done? Light-headed with anger, Kate rolled up her sleeves and prepared to attack the grimy cabin alone. "You'll regret this, Seth Hillerman," she muttered. "Just you wait."

Chapter Twenty

It seemed to take forever to bring *The Mary Ann* from the turning basin at the beginning of the canal through the closely spaced Georgetown locks the next morning. Kate held her breath as a loaded boat eased by, sandwiching her between the towpath and the line of boats moored along the wharf. She began to breathe normally again once the other boat had passed, but she didn't relax until the busy port was behind them.

"Put your harmonica away, Zeke, 'cause today I'm teaching you to steer," Kate said. "It's easy," she went on. "All you have to do is move the tiller in the opposite direction from the way you want the boat to go."

When Zeke looked bewildered, she said, "Let me show you. Here, take hold of this stick." Putting her hand over his, she pushed the tiller first to the right and then to the left. "See how it works?"

Zeke nodded, and eyes shining, he kept *The Mary Ann*

on course. Kate let him steer for more than an hour, until the next lock was in sight. After she blew the horn and hollered, "HE-EY, LOCK!" she turned to him and said, "You did a good job. I'll take over here so you can throw Seth the snubbing line." Now Seth couldn't accuse her of taking advantage of Zeke, Kate thought with satisfaction.

The canal stretched ahead of *The Mary Ann* in a gentle curve, the water a golden glare as it caught the last rays of the sun, and Kate felt at peace. She was glad to be away from Georgetown, glad to be past the congestion of the two groups of closely spaced locks—thirteen of them, altogether—that had raised them step by step until they were beyond Great Falls. Now they would make better time.

As Seth eased the tiller to the left, Kate turned to him and said, "By the way, you were right—Zeke can steer."

Seth's eyes widened. "Well, if *he's* going to steer, then *I'm* going to have a turn at being captain."

"That's what you think! There can only be one person in charge. One captain. Me."

Seth shook his head adamantly. "From now on, when I'm at the tiller, I'm the captain."

"Then from now on you won't be at the tiller. Zeke and I will steer, and you'll do all the chores."

"Now, wait a minute—"

"No, *you* wait a minute. I'm the captain and I always will be, and don't you forget it." Kate felt alert, poised to defend herself. No one was going to take away—or even share—her responsibility for Papa's boat and the mules.

Seth started to object, but before he could speak Kate raised the long tin horn to her lips and blew three resounding blasts.

Seth clapped his hands over his ears and said, "Okay,

okay! I'll let you be captain all the time if you promise not to deafen me like that again."

"Let" her be captain, indeed! The nerve of him, trying to turn all this into a joke. Rounding the curve, Kate saw that the lock tender had already opened the downstream gates so they could pull in, and by the time Seth had maneuvered the boat into position, she had decided what to do. After she threw Zeke the snubbing line, Kate turned to Seth and said, "I'll take over here. I want you to go ashore and tell Zeke I said for the two of you to switch places. For good."

"What's the big idea? I said you could be captain all the time, didn't I?"

"And I said for you to take over all Zeke's jobs." Kate watched Seth's expression of disbelief turn to anger and his hands ball into fists.

"I wish you really were a boy," Seth choked out, " 'cause if you were, I'd beat the tar out of you!"

Taken aback by his fury, Kate said, "Look, Seth, a captain—"

"A captain ought to be able to get through the tunnel without hiding in the cabin, but this has nothing to do with who will be the captain, and you know it, Kate. You're doing this to punish me for going into Washington City yesterday and 'cause you didn't like what I said about Zeke doing all the dirty work."

How dare Seth taunt her about her fear of the tunnel— that wasn't fair at all! The rage that had been smoldering deep inside Kate flared, and she burst out, "A person who thinks caring for the mules and keeping the boat spick-and-span is 'the dirty work' has no right to even think about being captain of a canal boat. And you know very well I'd never be unfair to Zeke."

"I must have forgotten that only mules and mutes can

152

expect decent treatment from you—Captain." Seth spat out the *captain* as if it were a curse.

Kate stared after him as he stormed off. She was shaken by the depth of his anger—and by his words. How dare he say she didn't treat people decently! In all her life, no one had ever before accused her of that. But then, the only people she'd ever treated badly were Seth and Julia.

Water was pouring into the lock chamber, splashing around the boat and raising it to the level of the canal ahead, and now Kate could see Seth standing beside Zeke while the older boy managed the snubbing line. Seth's back was toward her, but Zeke seemed to be listening intently. He glanced in Kate's direction, then nodded and handed over the line.

Kate's attention turned to Seth again, and she scowled. He was wrong. She wasn't being unfair, "punishing him," like he'd said—she was simply sticking up for herself. She was keeping him from taking over, protecting what was rightfully hers.

Slowly, the boat slipped out of the lock, and Zeke came to join Kate on the tiller deck. "Did Seth say that you and I would do all the steering from now on?" Zeke nodded, and his puzzled look told her that Seth had given him no explanation. "He wasn't very happy about the change, but I'm the captain, and I think it's the best thing to do."

Zeke nodded and reached for his harmonica. As he began to play, Kate's eyes turned to her stepbrother, walking beside General in the deepening dusk. To her surprise, she found that although she still smarted from what Seth had said, the terrible anger she'd felt toward him was gone, replaced by a feeling of betrayal. How could he taunt her about her fear of the tunnel *now* when he'd been so matter-of-fact about it at the time?

The tunnel. How was she going to face it again? Don't think

about it, Kate told herself. Just don't think about it. Shivering, she pulled her shawl tight around her shoulders.

The budding branches of the trees were silhouetted against a rosy twilight sky, and the canal reached into the distance like a black satin ribbon. Zeke came to the end of a song and Kate said, "It's time to light the bow lamp." She knew it wouldn't be any help to Seth since it lit only the waterway ahead of her, and she tried to imagine what it must be like to walk in the darkness. Driving the mules wouldn't be much fun if you couldn't see anything. Standing at the tiller certainly wasn't any fun at night.

A long silver ray shimmered on the canal just ahead of the boat, and Kate waited for Zeke to come back from lighting the lamp. He was company, even though he didn't speak. When he joined her, she said, "Play some more, Zeke," and moments later, strains of harmonica music filled the night air.

Far down the canal, Kate saw the light of a boat approaching them, and she watched the bright speck grow larger and larger. She steered closer to the berm, sensing that Seth had already stopped the mules on the river side of the towpath, allowing the towline to sink so the loaded boat could pass over it.

The driver of the boat's mule team, a boy about Seth's size, called a greeting as he went by, and Kate answered, then raised an arm to protect her eyes from the beam of the bow lamp. She lowered her arm as the other boat slipped past, and through its window she glimpsed a woman moving about the cabin. "Mrs. O'Malley," Kate whispered, recognizing Mama's friend from Williamsport.

Captain O'Malley spoke, his voice cheerful. "Hello on *The Mary Ann*," he said. "Is that you, Mrs. Betts? Or is that Katie at the tiller?"

"It's me, Captain," Kate said. "Mama's lying down inside.

And she's Mrs. Hillerman now, sir," she added, trying to sound pleased about it. The boat slid past, and Kate turned to follow it with her eyes as it faded into the night. The dim silhouette of the captain had showed one arm resting along the tiller, the other around a small child.

That was how it was supposed to be—the whole family together, with the father in charge of the boat and the mother in charge of everything else, the way it had been when Papa was alive. Boating wasn't supposed to be like this, with two twelve-year-olds on their own and a silent, childlike older boy to help them.

I miss you so much, Papa, Kate said silently, blinking back tears. Beside her, Zeke began to play again, and the plaintive sound of the harmonica matched Kate's mood. "Play something cheerful next, Zeke," she said, and he immediately changed to a rollicking nursery tune, one she recognized as a song Mama used to sing to her.

If only Mama were here now. If only she were just inside the cabin instead of back in Cumberland with Julia. An almost tangible sense of gloom settled over Kate as she imagined Julia taking Mama her breakfast tray each morning . . . Julia bringing Mama the first daffodils from the yard . . . ladylike little Julia sitting beside Mama in the evenings, making tiny stitches on her sampler.

Kate shivered in the cold darkness and wished she was back in Cumberland with her mother.

Chapter Twenty-One

An hour later Kate flexed her freezing fingers and said, "You can go to bed if you want to, Zeke." There was no reason for both of them to be out here in the cold.

Other evenings, she and Seth had kept each other company while Zeke walked this long, dark shift. Alone in the cold silence now, Kate felt small and forlorn. How had things gone so wrong between her and Seth? He was too proud to forgive her for letting Zeke take over at the tiller and giving him Zeke's chores—what he called "the dirty work"—and she would not forget his accusations. It was going to be a long trip home.

The light from *The Mary Ann's* bow lamp made a long, wavering beam on the water, but everything else was in darkness. It was so still that Kate could hear the creaking of the mules' harnesses and the jingling of their bells.

Soon, though, the night came alive with sound as the spring peepers filled the air with high-pitched trills that sounded like they were made by birds rather than frogs. Kate's spirits began to rise. She loved listening to the peepers. She had never seen one of the tiny tree frogs, but their piping was one of her favorite signs of spring. It lulled her now as she steered the boat through the darkness.

A volley of shots in the distance made the tree frogs fall silent, and for a moment, Kate was paralyzed by fear. But when she heard Zeke's footsteps on the hatch covers, her mind began to race. "Quick, Zeke, blow out the bow lamp!" she called as she steered the boat toward the berm. "Seth! Unhitch the mules and get them into the woods!"

The bow lamp went out, and Kate called, "Pull in the towline, Zeke." She heard Seth and the mules crashing about in the woods between the canal and the river, saw in her mind's eye Zeke pulling in the sodden line, hand over hand, hand over hand. And now one word—*Hurry!*— filled Kate's mind like a chant until above it she heard the beat of hooves.

"Get inside, Zeke—forget the line!" She flinched when the crack of a rifle firing was followed by another volley of shots, and then she heard Zeke running toward her across the hatch covers. *Hurry!*

The two of them practically fell into the cabin as the drumming of hoofbeats reached a crescendo. Zeke braced himself against the cabin door, but Kate ran to the window. Two groups of horsemen thundered past, darker shapes in the darkness, as shouts and more bursts of gunfire filled the night.

When it was quiet again, Kate drew a shaky breath and turned to Zeke, who was still pressed against the door. "They're gone now," she said, and as her fear began to ebb, she tried to decide what to do next.

Should they go on to the small settlement some distance ahead where they'd have the protection of Union troops, or should they get the mules to safety right away? That might be best, since she suddenly felt much too tired to steer the boat.

Maybe if Zeke drove the mules, Seth could steer and—No, Kate reminded herself, she wasn't letting Seth steer anymore. She scowled at the memory of his hateful words: *From now on, when I'm at the tiller, I'm the captain.* How dare he?

"Unload the team that's in the stable, Zeke," Kate said, "and then pole us across the canal so we can pick up Seth and bring his team over to the berm. I want the mules off the towpath tonight." She followed Zeke onto the tiller deck and called, "Hey, Seth—we're coming over to get you 'cause we're tying up here."

Kate heard the mules crashing through the woods again, and then Seth's voice came out of the darkness. "It's your decision, *Captain*, but—"

"That's right, it's my decision," Kate said shortly, but little fingers of uncertainty picked at her confidence. Was it the right decision? Of course it was, she told herself. If any Rebels were left after the Union troops were through with them, they'd be staying on their own side of the river for a while.

Kate headed for the cabin, longing to fall into bed and pull the quilt up over her head, but the way Seth had said "captain" troubled her. What a person said—or did—in the heat of anger was one thing, but this was something else. The idea of her stepbrother nursing his anger with every step he took in the cold darkness made her uneasy.

She'd make some cocoa, Kate decided. Seth loved cocoa, and besides, it would warm them and help them calm down. "Mama would make it for us if she were here now," Kate whispered as she turned wearily to the stove.

She had combined the ingredients and was heating the cocoa when Sandy brayed. Kate grabbed the lantern and ran outside, with Zeke at her heels. She shone the light along the berm where the mules were tethered, and it came to rest on a man—a short, ragged-looking man who was trying to shield his eyes against the light. "Get away from those mules," Kate said, her voice shaking.

"I'm—hurt," the man gasped. "I need—help." He rested a hand on Cupid's flank to steady himself, and the big mule turned away from the feed trough to look at him.

Seth's words came through the darkness. "I'm setting out the mule fall board. Hold that lantern to light his way to it."

Kate raised her voice to be heard above the noise of the fall board being put in place. "What are you talking about? You can't let that man on the boat!"

"He's in trouble," Seth said, edging along the race plank to reach for the lantern.

But Kate pulled it away. "Can't you see he's a Rebel? Besides—"

"Now don't you start in about how you're the captain, 'cause this doesn't have anything to do with boating."

"Then I'd like to know what it does have to do with," Kate said, her voice shrill.

"Decency. Human decency. Now give me the lantern." Holding it so the light shone on the fall board, Seth asked the man, "Can you manage that?"

"I'm—not sure," he gasped.

Kate saw Zeke look questioningly at Seth, and moments later the older boy was on the berm, moving the fall board so it leaned against the tiller deck and then half carrying the wounded Rebel aboard. When Kate saw the man's muddy boots, she knew he had reached the berm side by walking through a nearby culvert that carried a creek under the canal.

Suddenly, Kate became aware of the sound of hoofbeats.

Were the Rebels coming back? She stood as though rooted to the spot until Seth blew out the lantern and she heard his urgent whisper, "Get inside!"

A thin crescent of moon hung coldly just above the treetops now, giving barely enough light for Kate to see her way to the door. In the cabin, the wounded man sank into a chair at the table, and they all waited tensely as the hoofbeats grew louder and louder, then slowed to a stop. Kate was stumbling to the window to see whether the horsemen were Union soldiers or Rebels when a voice called, "Hello, on the boat!"

Kate heard the cabin door open and close, heard Seth call back, "Hello, on shore!" She was torn between helpless anger and guilty relief that her stepbrother had taken charge.

"We're looking for a Rebel raider we shot off his horse. You seen or heard anything suspicious?"

Union soldiers, then. Kate waited to hear what Seth would say.

"We heard horsemen ride by here a while ago."

"That was us, chasing the lot of 'em. Well, you shouldn't be bothered any more tonight. If you notice anything, let us know when you pass our camp tomorrow."

Kate let the curtain fall back over the window. Human decency or not, this was wartime, and the Rebels were the enemy. If Seth wouldn't turn the man in, she would. She'd have no qualms about taking care of that when they stopped to lock through at Seneca in the morning.

Seth came back inside and Kate said, "You'd better take care of your patient. The water in the kettle is hot."

A horrified look crossed her stepbrother's face when his eyes fell on the man's blood-soaked sleeve, and he swallowed hard. He glanced at Zeke, who pointed to himself and nodded.

Kate took the scissors from the shelf. "You'll have to cut off his sleeve," she said, handing Zeke the scissors.

Nodding, Zeke set to work. As he cut the bloodstained cloth away from the man's wound, Kate thought of how he had clipped the hairs away from the hurt place on Sandy's leg, remembered how quickly the cut had healed.

Zeke glanced at the fuel can, and Kate brought it to him. Did he understand that pouring kerosene on a wound would keep it from becoming infected, or was he just doing what he'd seen his mother do when someone was hurt? Doing what he did when a mule was hurt?

The Rebel moaned, and from the corner of her eye, Kate saw Seth stumble to the window. She didn't want to be squeamish like her stepbrother, but the smell of the kerosene combined with the sight of mangled flesh made her queasy, and she turned away. "Zeke's going to need bandages," she said. "We'd better tear some strips from your sheet, Seth."

Zeke had barely finished binding the Rebel's arm when Kate heard voices and knew that more men had come through the culvert under the canal bed. Were they Union soldiers who would discover them helping an enemy— wasn't that treason?—or had the Rebel raiders come back? Kate waited, her heart thumping against her ribs. If only she'd decided to go on instead of tying up here!

Footsteps clumped across the hatch covers, and a voice said, "Wait a minute with that kerosene—I'll spread some hay around and then you can douse it good."

"Right," came the reply. "Adams, you get the people off of here so we can fire the boat, and Jones, you untie those mules."

Someone banged on the back wall of the cabin and called, "Everybody out—we're gonna burn this tub." This wasn't happening, Kate thought. How could she bear to lose *The Mary Ann* and the mules, especially Cupid? Now everything she cared about would be gone. Oh, Papa, Papa! she cried silently, I was trying to help!

One of the Rebel raiders yanked the cabin door open and growled, "All right, everybody outside! You first, sonny," he said, pointing at Kate, who had sprung to her feet.

Suddenly her arms and legs felt heavy, so heavy they seemed to pull her downward instead of moving her forward, and the cabin was growing dim even though no one had touched the lamp. Dimmer still, then dark. Dark and still. Then, as though from a great distance, came a confusion of sounds, and Kate opened her eyes to find herself sprawled on Seth's mattress and the cabin filled with Rebel raiders, all of them crowded around the wounded man.

"We were sure the Yankees had you, Jacobs," someone said.

Kate blinked and sat up as a man who seemed to be the leader opened the door and said, "What's going on in here? We don't have all night." Then his eyes widened and he said, "Jacobs! We figured you were a goner! Adams, take him on your horse and start back while the rest of us get everybody off and set this boat afire."

But the wounded man—Jacobs—said, "Hold on a minute, now. These boys didn't turn me over to the Yankees when they had the chance, and this big fellow here has probably saved my right arm. I can't let you burn 'em out."

Filled with hope, Kate whispered, "Please. Oh, please."

The leader asked, "Have you forgotten that Federal warships run on the coal these boats haul to Georgetown?" His voice was cold, but Jacobs held his ground.

"I'm not talking about the war," he said, and echoing what Seth had said earlier, he added, "I'm talking about human decency." The wounded Rebel flashed Kate a meaningful glance, and she felt her color rising.

One of the older raiders broke the sudden silence. "Jacobs is right," he said quietly. "Besides, we don't make war on children. Let's go." He led the others outside, and Kate crept to the tiller deck to watch them help the wounded man ashore. She stood and stared into the darkness until she heard the stamping of horses as they mounted, heard the leader call something to them before they rode off.

"What did he say?" Kate asked.

"That we'd better tether our mules again so they don't stray."

Wiping away tears of relief, Kate said, "I'll do it," and revived by the cold air, she went down the fall board to fling her arms around Cupid's neck. She rested her cheek against the mule's warm shoulder for a moment of comfort, and then she whispered, "Now, let's get you tied up again."

As Kate was fumbling for the rope, a ray of light shone down, and when she had the mules securely tethered, it guided her back to the boat. After she came aboard, Zeke handed her the lantern and headed for the hay house.

"Thanks, Zeke," she called after him, but he made no sign that he had heard. He must be angry because her decision to tie up here had put them in danger, Kate thought. She walked toward the cabin, sure that nothing Seth could say would be worse than Zeke's silent reproach. Steeling herself, she opened the door.

Seth had just finished pouring coal into the stove, and as Kate came inside he pointed at the steaming pan. "We forgot all about the cocoa. I can take Zeke's out to him, if you want."

Kate nodded, not trusting herself to speak. She lifted off the brownish skin that had formed over the surface of the steaming liquid and then filled three cups, trying to ignore the smell of scorched milk. As she filled the pan with cold water, she saw that a dark, lacelike pattern was burned onto the bottom.

When Seth came back from the hay house and sat down across the small table from Kate she looked up and said, "I made the wrong decision. We should have gone on and tied up at Seneca, where the army camp is." Go ahead and say it, she cried silently. Go ahead and say that I don't deserve to be the captain.

"The raiders probably would have caught up to us before we got there," Seth said, "and we wouldn't have had Jacobs to speak out for us. I'm just glad it's all over with and that things turned out the way they did."

"I think I'd have died if they'd taken the mules," Kate said, deciding that fear of the Rebels must have made Seth forget his anger toward her.

"It sure would have been a long walk home."

Kate said quietly, "It's *still* going to be a long walk home."

"Listen, Kate, I don't think we ought to tell your mother about what happened tonight."

"Neither do I. If she knew, she'd wouldn't let us make another trip." Kate didn't intend to let the Rebels scare her off the waterway—not when boating was the only way to earn the money Mama needed. The only way without renting out *The Mary Ann* and the mules.

"What I meant," Seth said stiffly, "is that we shouldn't worry her."

Our whole trip has worried her, Kate thought guiltily. "This cocoa tastes scorched," she said, pushing her cup away. "I'm going to bed."

Chapter Twenty-Two

Mist hung low above the canal and river the next morning, and it made Kate feel safely hidden. Protected. Even though she shivered as the dampness clung to her clothes, she was almost sorry when the sun burned off the mist. But the brilliance of the sky seemed to give her new energy, and Kate's spirits rose as she filled her lungs with the fresh spring air.

And then she saw the horseshoe prints in a sandy spot on the towpath. Forced to think about the night before, Kate shuddered, and her hand stole to Cupid's shoulder. If Seth hadn't taken over and helped the wounded raider, the burned-out hull of *The Mary Ann* would be blocking the canal and the mules would be on their way to join some Rebel wagon train. To think that if Seth had listened to her, if he had obeyed her because she was the captain, everything that was important to her would be gone.

"Tee, yip, YA-ah!"

Seth's call brought Kate out of her reverie, and she saw a loaded boat approaching. She maneuvered her team to the river side of the towpath before she stopped them, embarrassed that she hadn't been aware of the downstream boat. Her spirits rose when she recognized *The Betty* and an instant later saw her friends Sally and Sue sitting on the cabin roof with their bare feet dangling. Kate was about to shout a greeting when she remembered that this morning she was the hired driver "Nate."

"Any news?" called *The Betty*'s mule driver, the girls' brother Paul.

Pitching her voice a little lower, Kate called back, "Heard our cavalry chasin' after some Rebel raiders last night. Both sides fired some shots." She pulled her straw hat forward a little and pretended to be checking Cupid's harness until the other boat had passed. She hoped she'd be wearing a dress the next time they met *The Betty* so she could chat with her friends.

Later, when they approached the next lock, Kate stopped the mules again to trade places with Zeke so she could lock the boat through. It had been a lot simpler when Seth steered, she thought as she waited for *The Mary Ann* to drift toward shore.

As soon as she took her place at the tiller, Kate blew the horn and shouted, "HE-EY, LOCK!" Seth came out of the stable, and Kate waited for him to say that he should steer again so she wouldn't have to get on and off the boat to lock them through on her shift as mule driver. But to her surprise, he just picked up the snubbing line and waited to toss it to Zeke.

As the rising water in the lock lifted the boat to the next level, she remembered that this was where she'd planned to turn in the wounded Rebel raider. To think that the man she would have betrayed had saved the boat and the mules for her! Or rather, for Seth and Zeke, who had helped him.

Trying to forget the night before, Kate concentrated on watching one of the young soldiers on the warehouse wharf, but she soon found herself wondering whether he had been with the horsemen who chased the raiders. She was glad when the boat was under way again and Seth joined her on the tiller deck.

"The lock tender told me that not a single man from the Seneca camp was even scratched last night," he said. "Looks like our wounded Rebel was the only one hit in all that shooting."

"You mean *your* wounded Rebel. Look, it turned out to be a good thing for us that you let him on board, so I'm glad you did. But I still don't see why you would want to help an enemy."

After a moment Seth said, "When he came to us asking for help, he was just a man in trouble, Kate, and I couldn't turn away someone in trouble. I couldn't turn him over to the soldiers once he was counting on us to help him, either. It wouldn't have been right."

"Even though you knew he would shoot your own father if he had the chance?" Kate challenged. "Or didn't you think about your father?"

"I think about him all the time," Seth said, staring straight ahead. "It was because of my father that I had to help that man," he added quietly.

Kate echoed, "Because of your father? What on earth are you talking about?"

"The night before he left, Papa asked me to promise that I'd always do what I knew was right, no matter how hard it was," Seth said, "and I have to keep my promise."

Kate understood immediately. "I'm glad you told me," she said honestly. That explained not just why Seth had helped the wounded Rebel, but also why he had always treated her decently—except for last evening when he taunted her about the tunnel. Kate's hand tightened on the tiller. She didn't want to think about the tunnel, and she didn't want to think about Seth's seething rage, either. "Look," she said, pointing. "The mayapples are in bloom."

Chapter Twenty-Three

"I wonder what's the matter up ahead," Seth said as *The Mary Ann* approached a series of closely spaced locks two days later.

"I think it's just heavy traffic," Kate said, frowning when she saw a boat in the lock and another in line ahead of them. She glanced at the lowering gray sky and thought the day seemed more like November than April. "It's almost noon, so as long as we're stopped, I might as well heat some soup to warm us up," she said.

As Kate filled the firebox of the stove with corncobs to make a quick, hot fire, she thought wistfully of last year and the years before when delays at locks meant a chance to chat with the other boaters. Now, though, it seemed safer to have as little as possible to do with people along the waterway—even when she was wearing a dress.

Kate was slicing the loaf of bread she'd bought the afternoon before when she heard a commotion outside. Curious, she set down her knife, gave the soup a stir, and went outside. She looked up the towpath and saw a crowd of small boys gathered around Zeke, yelling taunts and pelting him with pebbles.

"How dare they!" Kate cried, hurrying to the bow. But Seth got there first and took charge.

"Hey!" he called. "If you boys know what's good for you, you'll leave him alone. His father doesn't take kindly to folks who pester him—and neither do I." His voice had a threatening tone Kate had never heard before, and the boys hesitated, then dropped their stones and sheepishly headed toward the lock house.

Zeke gave Seth a grateful look before he hunched his shoulders and put his hands in his pockets. Kate couldn't stand that hangdog look, couldn't stand the idea of the other boaters seeing Zeke like that. "Come on over here," she called. "We're about to eat."

As Zeke came aboard, Kate scolded, "You've got to learn to stick up for yourself, Zeke. I'd rather see you toss those troublemakers in the canal than just stand there and let them pick on you."

Zeke hung his head and started toward the hay house. Kate hurried after him, chagrined that she had made him feel even worse, but he shut himself inside and wouldn't respond to her knock. "Come on out," she said, "or your soup will be cold."

"I'll take it to him," Seth called. "Can't you see he wants to be left alone?"

It didn't feel right to be sitting at the table without Zeke, and Kate was glad when the hurried meal was over. By the time they finished, it was their turn to lock through, and soon they were on their way again with Zeke driving the mules as though nothing had happened.

A loaded boat was approaching, and Kate recognized

the *Pride of the Waterway*, with the boating family's small children tethered to a ring in the center of the cabin's flat roof so they wouldn't fall overboard. She remembered when she'd ridden like that, playing safely in the shade of the canvas awning.

As the boat passed, the captain's wife waved and called, "How's your Mama, Katie? I hear she's married again."

"She's been feeling poorly lately," Kate called back.

A knowing expression crossed the woman's face, and Kate thought, She's guessed about the baby. Turning to Seth, she said, "I don't see how you can be so nice to Julia when it's her fault your mother died."

Seth looked shocked. "How can you say it was Julia's fault? It was just something that happened."

"Still, it happened because of Julia. I'd never forgive your father if Mama died having his baby." As soon as she spoke, Kate regretted her words, but before she had a chance to take them back, Seth lashed out at her.

"And if she doesn't die, you'll never forgive him for marrying her, you'll never forgive Julia for wanting a mother, you'll never forgive the baby for being born, and you'll never forgive me for— What is it you have against me, Kate? I've never been sure." When she didn't answer, he prompted, "Is it not knowing as much as you do about boating, or is it catching on to it faster than you thought I would?"

Kate stared at Seth's flushed face and eyes that smoldered with anger, and for once she was speechless.

"What's the matter, Kate?" Seth challenged. "Does the truth hurt?"

Finding her voice, Kate said, "You haven't caught on all that well to taking care of the mules. Zeke does a lot better with them than you do."

Seth shrugged and said, "You're the one who had us trade jobs."

He was right, Kate thought. "Well, the mules are your responsibility now," she said lamely.

Seth hollered for Zeke to stop, and Kate cried, "Just what do you think you're doing?"

"Trading shifts with Zeke."

Raising her voice, Kate called, "Go on, Zeke, we're not stopping." Then she turned to Seth and said, "Don't you *ever* do that again!"

"Do *what* again?"

"Try to take over! Make decisions that the captain's supposed to make!" Kate's voice shook, and Seth stared at her as though he thought she was crazy. Kate felt her face grow warm as she realized he hadn't been trying to take over at all. He just wanted to get away from her.

I hate him, hate him, hate him! Kate cried silently as her stepbrother gave an exaggerated shrug and disappeared into the cabin, slamming the door. How dare he talk to her like that? What gave him the right to tell her— *To tell her the truth*. Kate's shoulders slumped. Everything Seth had said was true, and the truth *did* hurt.

Kate steered closer to the berm to let a loaded boat pass. Seth really *had* caught on to boating, she thought, and that was why he'd gotten too big for his britches and tried to take over. That, and saving her from the sailor in Georgetown. Kate scowled, remembering how later that day Seth had practically accused her of being unfair to Zeke. How he'd gone off without helping to clean the boat. Before that, they'd been getting along better than she'd thought possible. She'd even started to like him, and she hadn't been mean to him for a long time.

And thanks to his promise to his father, Seth had never really been mean to her, Kate mused. He'd challenged her sometimes, like he had just now, but he'd never said anything she didn't deserve. His father would be proud of the way Seth was keeping his promise.

And Papa would be proud of the way she remembered everything he'd taught her about boating, Kate told herself. But then she was struck by a terrible truth: She might have remembered everything Papa taught her about boating, but she'd forgotten almost everything he'd taught her about life. Papa would be proud of Captain Kate, but he would wonder what had become of his Katie.

The memory of how she'd behaved during the past six months filled Kate with remorse. Papa would be so disappointed in her! No, he'd be ashamed. "Oh, Papa," Kate whispered, her eyes blurred with tears, "I'm sorry. From now on I'll do better, I promise I will."

Chapter Twenty-Four

At midmorning the next day, Kate steered into the basin at one of larger towns along the canal. Making her way to the bow of the boat, she opened the stable door and told Seth, "I need you to have the hay house filled while I buy groceries." His only response was to put away the small metal pick he'd been using to remove pebbles from the mules' hooves.

"Have the cost put on our account," Kate added, turning away. Even though she'd pretended not to notice his silence at supper last night and breakfast today, she knew she hadn't fooled him—or Zeke, either.

This morning, Zeke had looked from her to Seth, his face puzzled at first and then sad. Maybe she had imagined it, but Kate was almost positive that she'd seen reproach in the older boy's eyes before he turned and followed Seth out of the cabin. Why did he blame *her?*

As she made her way to the cabin to get the money

for her shopping trip, Kate decided that she'd much rather face Seth's angry words than his stony silence. She could defend herself against what he said. Besides, how could she do better if he never talked to her? If he never gave her another chance?

Kate had just slipped some coins into her pocket when she had an idea that brought a smile to her face, and taking a tablet and pencil from the small drawer in the table, she sat down and began to write.

Five minutes later, she pulled the cabin door shut behind her and called cheerfully, "Come along, Zeke—you can help me carry the groceries."

When they returned to the boat with their supplies, Kate found Seth standing at the table, the tablet in his hand. "I—I'm sorry, Kate. I thought you'd left a note for me," he said as he handed it to her. "I didn't mean to read your letter."

"That's all right—I left it there so you would," Kate said. "I couldn't figure out any other way to let you know I'd thought about what you said yesterday." And not only had her ruse worked, it had forced Seth to break his silence, too.

He frowned and took back the tablet. "I guess you must mean this part—'Hope you are feeling all right and that you have gotten a letter from my stepfather by now. Tell Julia hello for me,'" he read, his tone dubious.

"That's the part," Kate said evenly, determined not to give him any excuse to go into his silent act again. She reached for the tablet and tore off the page. Slipping the letter into an envelope she'd addressed earlier, Kate asked, "Do you mind mailing this while I put the groceries away? I'll give you money for the stamp," she added as she reached into her pocket for a coin.

Zeke followed Seth from the cabin, and Kate's heart

was heavy as she watched him go. When had Zeke become Seth's shadow instead of hers? Was it the day she scolded him for not sticking up for himself when the younger boys pestered him? No, the change in Zeke had come before that. But when?

Kate closed her eyes and tried to remember. Sorting through her memories of the past week, she saw Zeke holding the lantern to light her way while she tethered the mules after the raiders left, saw him turn away without meeting her eyes. "It's because I didn't want to help the wounded Rebel!" Kate exclaimed. *Zeke was disappointed in her.*

It was all too complicated for someone like Zeke to understand, Kate told herself as she put away the wedge of cheese she'd bought. He didn't understand about the war. About enemies. He'd just seen that the man was hurt, and he'd wanted to help him.

Zeke had *wanted* to help, and Seth had known he *ought* to help, but her impulse was to turn the man away. To let him suffer because he was a Rebel. What was it Papa used to say? Kate closed her eyes again and tried to remember. It was something about how rich or poor, man or woman, immigrant or American born, in spite of their differences, all people had the same worth because—

Kate's eyes popped open and she rushed from the cabin calling to Zeke. He came out of the hay house and hurried toward her, a questioning look on his face. "I was wrong when I didn't want to let that Rebel raider come on board the other night," Kate said. "You and Seth did the right thing to help him."

A broad smile lit up Zeke's face, and Kate smiled back. Not a mean bone in his body, she thought, remembering what Mrs. Connally had said about her son. "I guess my whole skeleton is mean," Kate muttered as she opened the cabin door, not liking that idea at all. Zeke was kind, but she was—mean.

Sometimes we can learn from a person like Zeke, Papa had said. And when he'd seen that she was puzzled, he'd added, *We can learn what is important in life.* Then, she had just assumed he meant being able to speak, but now she understood. Kate's head began to ache. Yesterday Seth had told her some hard truths about herself, and today Zeke—without even knowing it—had made her face up to another.

Kate sighed and began to put away the rest of the groceries. She was setting a tin of tea on the shelf when her stepbrother came into the cabin a few minutes later, with Zeke at his heels. "I mailed your letter," Seth said.

"Thanks. I'll be ready to leave in just a minute." Kate turned around when Zeke tapped her on the shoulder. He pointed first to her, then to himself, and then he pointed to her again and to Seth.

Frowning, Kate said, "I'm sorry, Zeke, but I don't know what you mean." With exaggerated movements, he repeated the motions and looked at her expectantly, but Kate was no less bewildered. What was he trying to tell her?

Zeke hesitated for a moment, then beckoned to her and went out the cabin door. Kate and Seth followed him until he motioned for them to stop, and they watched him disappear into the hay house. They were exchanging puzzled glances when Zeke burst out of the hay house and ran toward Kate, stopping in front of her with his hand cupped around his ear as if he were listening.

Now Kate understood. "You want me to tell Seth what I said to you a little while ago?" His face wreathed in smiles, Zeke nodded, and Kate turned to her stepbrother. "I told Zeke I was wrong not to let that wounded Rebel on board the other night, and he wants me to tell you, too." She hesitated, and then went on in a rush, "And I only said what I did yesterday because I was angry. It isn't true."

"*What* isn't true?"

Kate felt her cheeks burn, but she didn't really blame Seth for making her say it right out, and she forced herself to meet his eyes. "It isn't true that you don't do a good job with the mules. You do fine." Zeke nodded in vigorous agreement, and Seth looked pleased.

Kate thought back to the angry challenge her step-brother had flung at her the day before. He *had* caught on to boating a lot faster than she'd thought he would, and that *was* what she had against him. No, that was too strong. She didn't hold it against him, but it made her uneasy. It kept her on guard.

"We'd better get under way," Seth said, breaking into her thoughts.

"Pole us over to the towpath so I can get off, Zeke," Kate said, " 'cause its your turn to steer the boat for a while."

As Kate walked along beside the mules, she muttered, "I have to share Mama with a stepfamily, and I have to share my room with Julia, but I'm not going to share being captain." Glancing back at Zeke, who was proudly holding the boat on course, Kate added silently, Still, I don't have to be mean about it.

Chapter Twenty-Five

After breakfast the next morning Kate said, "We have to stop at the first town we come to, because I forgot to buy oatmeal yesterday." Ignoring the face Seth made as he poured hot water from the teakettle into the dishpan, Kate wrapped herself in her shawl and went out into the April sunshine.

Oatmeal with brown sugar and the cream that rose to the top of the milk pitcher had always been her favorite breakfast, and she enjoyed it even more now that she didn't have to wash the gummy pan the oatmeal was cooked in. Was that pan the reason Seth made a face?

Kate pushed the boat away from the berm with the pole and made her way to the tiller. Morning was the best part of the day, she thought as the boat passed two deer browsing at the water's edge.

An hour later Kate was steering the drifting boat into the basin of a small canalside village when she heard a child's terrified cries, and to her horror, she saw Zeke holding a small boy over the water. "Stop!" she cried. Zeke looked across at her, a puzzled expression on his face, while the child squirmed and cried out for mercy. "Put him down on the bank," Kate called.

The little boy took off down the towpath as soon as his feet touched the ground, and to Kate's great relief, no one seemed to have witnessed what had happened. A small group of curious children began to gather in front of the store, and one of them asked, "Why was Willy hollerin'?"

From the stable door, Seth said, "We don't know anybody named Willy." Raising his voice, he called, "Get those mules moving again, Zeke—we aren't stopping here after all." Once they had left the basin, Seth asked Kate, "What got into him all of a sudden? After the way he just stood and let those boys badger him the other day, it doesn't make sense."

"I guess it's my fault," Kate admitted, and she told Seth what she'd said to Zeke after they'd rescued him from the boys who had surrounded him two days before. "I'll have to be more careful what I say," she added.

"You'd better be. But for now, I'll go talk to him man to man about what he should ignore and when he should stick up for himself." Kate steered the boat toward the bank, and Seth set the plank in place and went ashore. As she pulled the plank back on board, Kate watched him run to catch up with Zeke, half glad that he'd taken charge, half resentful. " 'Man to man,' indeed," she said.

Back at the tiller she told herself, Well, no harm's done, and we can buy our oatmeal somewhere else. But harm *had* been done, she thought, remembering Zeke's bewildered expression, and it had been her fault. It would have been her fault if that child had drowned, too. Zeke was simply doing exactly what she'd told him, just as he had the day he'd stayed inside the smoke-filled cabin while she and Seth were away.

Kate felt a sense of heaviness, almost as though huge hands were bearing down on her shoulders. Her careless comment to Zeke wasn't the first time she'd shown poor judgment on this trip. She had to do better—a captain couldn't afford to make mistakes.

"In a mile or so, we'll go by the lock Zeke's father tends," Kate announced that afternoon, moving the tiller a little to the left.

"I hope Zeke will want to go on with us instead of staying home. It sure is easier with three people on the crew."

"He'll stay with us," Kate said confidently, "and that will make Mama feel a lot better about letting us make another trip."

Frowning, Seth asked, "Are you sure you want to do this again, Kate?"

Kate wasn't at all sure she did, but she wasn't going to let anybody know that. "We have to do it again, whether we want to or not, Seth."

"I don't think your mother will let us."

"She'll have to let us," Kate said quietly. "She needs the money. Besides, once we've made it to Georgetown and back, Mama can't very well say it isn't possible, can she?"

After another pause Seth said, "Maybe by now the government's paid the army and my father's sent the money home."

"You really don't want to go again, do you?"

"I never wanted to go in the first place, not that it made any difference to you."

"Well," Kate said, determined not to lose her temper, "you've been a good sport, and you've done a good job, too. Zeke and I might be able to manage without you, but it wouldn't be the same." It wasn't a lie, Kate told herself. She'd said they *might* be able to manage, hadn't she?

"Zeke would do whatever you told him to, and he'd never ask to be the captain. You'd like that."

Seth sounded like he really wasn't going to make another trip.

"Hey, has the cat got your tongue?"

"I'm trying to think of a way to convince you to stay with *The Mary Ann*."

"Why don't you just ask me to?"

Surprised, Kate turned to him. "Would you stay? I—I don't think I could do it without you."

"I know you couldn't. Besides, your mother would never let you go unless I was along."

"You mean she'd never let you stay in Cumberland while I went down the waterway."

"That, too," Seth acknowledged.

Kate frowned, wondering why it was no longer fun to make Seth give in to her, wondering why she was almost dreading the rest of boating season. Oh, Papa, she mourned, boating just isn't the same without you and Mama here with me. It used to be such fun, but now it's nothing but work, work, work.

Ten minutes later, Kate raised the horn to her lips and blew three notes, then yelled "HE-EY, LOCK!" for good measure.

"I hope you're right that Zeke's going to want to stay with us," Seth said. "He sure looks eager to get home."

Kate had already noticed the brisk pace Zeke had set for the mules, noticed the extra spring in his step as they neared his home. He *has* to stay with us, she said silently, 'cause we can't manage without him.

When the lock house came in sight, Kate saw Mrs.

Connally waiting in the yard, heard her call, "He's back!" and watched her hurry to the towpath and run toward her son.

"I don't think Mrs. Connally is going to want him to stay with us," Seth said, sounding glum.

Kate watched the little woman throw her arms around her tall son, saw him lift her off her feet in a bear hug. Longing for her own mother, Kate's eyes filled with tears. It had been so long since she'd felt Mama's arms around her—so long since she'd *let* Mama hug her.

As the boat drifted forward, Kate watched Zeke set his mother back on her feet and snap his fingers for the mules to start up again. Mrs. Connally walked beside her son and watched proudly as he caught the line Seth tossed him, looped it around the snubbing post, and brought *The Mary Ann* to a smooth stop.

"Zeke was a big help to us, Mr. Connally," Kate said as the lock tender closed the heavy gates behind her. "We'd like to keep him as part of our crew."

For a moment, Mr. Connally didn't answer, his eyes on his wife and youngest son. "His ma, she missed him something terrible. Been comin' out and lookin' downstream every time she heard a horn blow for the past two or three days. But we already talked about it, and she says it's for him to decide."

Raising her voice above the sound of the water rushing into the lock, Kate said, "I hope he decides to stay." But as the boat slowly rose, she saw that Seth had taken Zeke's place at the snubbing post and Zeke was nowhere in sight.

"Tie up on the berm side and put your mules in our pasture, Katie," Mrs. Connally called. "We'll have a good visit, and the three of you can be on your way in the morning."

The three of us! "Are you sure Zeke wants to stay with *The Mary Ann?*" Kate asked, hoping against hope.

Mrs. Connally smiled wistfully. "I'm almost positive," she said. "He's always wanted to go down the waterway, and there's been captains asking to take him on, but nobody I could trust to treat him right. Nobody I was sure wouldn't take advantage of the way he is, wouldn't make sport of him. Until now."

"Well, I'm glad you trusted Seth and me enough to let Zeke come with us. I don't think we'd ever have gotten to Georgetown without him," Kate said as the lock gates opened ahead of her. Her spirits rose at the thought of their stopover with the Connallys—a chance to visit and catch up on the news, and two meals she wouldn't have to cook. Two meals that wouldn't be either bean soup or oatmeal.

Chapter Twenty-Six

Kate squinted into the afternoon sun until it was hidden by the bulk of the mountain rising ahead of her. Carefully, she angled the boat into the narrow, rocky cut that led to the tunnel, dreading the sight of its gaping portal. She was sure her face must be almost as pale as Julia's.

"You don't have to do this, Kate," Seth said, sounding worried. "Forget what I said the other night—I never would have said a thing like that if I hadn't been so angry."

Without looking at him, Kate said flatly, "What you said was true. A canal boat captain ought to be able to go through the tunnel without hiding in the cabin." *I never ask my crew to do anything I wouldn't be willing to do myself.* How many times had she heard Papa say that?

Kate swallowed hard. She would steer the boat through Paw Paw Tunnel today, and on the next trip, she would walk through the tunnel with the mules. After that, there wouldn't be any question about who should be the captain.

"Hey, how come we're slowing down?" Seth asked.

As Kate steered the drifting boat around the sharp curve she saw the mules stopped just outside the tunnel portal and Zeke running toward the boat. She divided her attention between managing *The Mary Ann* and trying to reassure Zeke.

"This is the tunnel I told you about," she said. "It's pretty long, but once you get inside you can see through it to the other end." Leaving the tiller, she said, "I'll light the bow lamp, and then you'll be able to see the railing that goes all along the ledge where you'll walk." Where I'll have to walk next time, she added silently.

While she talked, Kate hurried to the bow, noticing how the air grew cooler as she came closer to the tunnel. When she had lit the lamp, shivering at the sight of the ghostly shadows it cast on the tunnel's arched walls, she saw that Zeke hadn't moved and that his face had a closed, stubborn look.

Kate's shoulders sagged. "Oh, all right, Zeke, come aboard," she said, putting out the plank. "I'll have Seth drive the mules."

Zeke was on board in a flash, and he disappeared into the hay house just as Seth hollered from the stern, "Boat coming! Somebody get those mules moving!"

Kate was off the boat in an instant, running toward the team, yelling, "COME up!" Even after the driver stopped his mules, that boat would drift forward several lengths. What if it hit them and pushed *The Mary Ann* into the face of the cliff that rose to the right of the tunnel's mouth?

Here, where the mountain had been blasted away to build the canal, the towpath was a boardwalk, and Kate's footsteps echoed on the wooden planks as she raced along it. Grabbing Cupid's bridle, she pulled the reluctant mules ahead at a trot until they were stopped short at the end of the towline.

"COME up! COME up!" she urged. Her heart beat wildly as the mules leaned forward. L-e-a-n, step. L-e-a-n, step, step. Now the boat was under way again, and the mules were pulling steadily, pulling *The Mary Ann* into the tunnel. Beside them, Kate felt the cool dampness close around her as the light grew dimmer and dimmer. *What was she doing here in this terrible place?*

Kate's mouth was dry and her breath came in gasps. They were so far into the tunnel now that all daylight was gone. The beam of the bow lamp wavered on the dark water and highlighted the curving walls and arched ceiling well ahead of Kate, but beyond its reach, murky darkness stretched all the way to the distant patch of light that was the upstream portal. The worst thing, though, was not being able to see the towpath.

What if there were rats in the tunnel? What if there were *snakes*? Two days ago, she had seen a small green snake in the grass along the towpath. Kate gasped as water dripping from the tunnel's ceiling splashed on her arm. She couldn't stand this much longer. When would she be out of here?

Above the pounding in her head, Kate heard Seth call her name, and when she looked back, shielding her eyes against the glare of the bow lamp, she saw that he had lit a lantern and hung it on the pole. Leaving the mules, she groped her way toward the boat, both hands on the wooden railing that edged the towpath. At last she reached up to catch the lantern as it slid along the pole.

With one hand on the rail and one gripping the curved wire handle of the lantern, Kate hurried back to the mules. The lantern swung crazily, its light bouncing off the tunnel's brick walls and ceiling. "COME up," she gasped when she caught up to the team. Junior tossed his head and brayed as she passed him, and the sound echoed, bouncing from side to side like fiendish laughter. Totally unnerved, Kate clung to one of the leather straps on Cupid's harness.

The lantern bobbed about, its light beaming in all directions, making it hard for Kate to keep her equilibrium, and the echo of the mules' hooves made it sound as if she were being pursued by a stampeding herd. And now, responding to her fear, the mules bolted forward, and Kate was nearly dragged off her feet. "Whoa," she gasped as the lantern fell and shattered, flickering out. "Whoa!" But the mules didn't stop.

Panic-stricken, Kate clung to the strap with both hands as the frightened animals pulled her along. Suddenly the tunnel was plunged into total darkness. Seth had blown out the bow lamp! Junior brayed again, and this time Cupid answered. The sound reverberated as the mules slowed to a stop. Slumping against Cupid, Kate could feel the big animal trembling.

Behind her, Kate heard Seth's anxious voice call, "Are you all right? Should I light the bow lamp again?"

She drew a shaky breath and called back, "I—I'm fine, and you can light the lamp." It was lucky for her that Seth had blown it out, Kate realized as she stroked Cupid, both comforting and being comforted. She wouldn't have thought to do that, wouldn't have guessed that darkness would halt the runaways. Kate tried not to think of what would have happened if she'd stumbled and fallen under the hooves of the frightened mules—or become tangled in their harness.

When the beam of light cut through the blackness again, Kate gave Cupid one last pat. "COME up," she coaxed, her voice trembling, and then she straightened her shoulders and commanded, "COME up!"

The mules moved forward, and Kate concentrated on the patch of light ahead of her. "One step and then another, and the longest journey's done," she recited. "One step and then another . . ."

Kate had no idea how many times she'd chanted those words before she noticed the darkness beginning to lift. Surrounded by deep gray instead of dusky black, she felt as though a weight was slowly being eased from her shoulders. And just ahead was the upstream portal, so close that she could see through its arch to a loaded boat waiting its turn.

Now, fingers of daylight reached into the tunnel. She was almost out. She'd done it! She could hardly wait to tell Mama—and to tell her how that verse of the "One step and then another" poem had helped.

When Kate stepped out of the tunnel into the sunlight at last, she felt as though she was waking from a nightmare.

"Have a little trouble in there, sonny? Hey, I'm asking you something!"

"Sorry, mister," Kate said, finally understanding that she was the "sonny" the other driver was speaking to. "These mules don't much like the tunnel. My brother had to blow out the bow lamp to get 'em to calm down."

Surprised at how natural it felt to say "brother," Kate watched *The Mary Ann* ease through the portal. She flashed Seth a triumphant look and decided that the expression on his face was a mixture of concern and respect. Mostly respect.

Kate waved a greeting to the captain of the loaded boat as she stepped over its towline, and with a pang, she saw that he was one of Papa's friends, a man who had spent many evenings at their table, playing cribbage. Did the captain ever think of Papa? Did he still miss him? Mama didn't. "At least I don't think she does," Kate whispered, "but I do."

A few minutes later a horn blew, and Kate stopped the mules so the boat that had followed them through the tunnel could go by. As its driver came toward her he called, "I took care of the broken glass from your lantern, sonny."

Kate thanked him, sure that she was blushing scarlet. How could she not have thought of the danger that broken glass would pose? Too embarrassed to meet the captain's eyes when he passed, she was grateful that it would be "some boy driving for *The Mary Ann*" and not Kate Betts who would be the villain when the story of her frightened passage through the tunnel was told.

"Wait a minute before you start the mules," Seth called, and when Kate glanced back, she saw that he was poling the boat over to the towpath. She waited while Zeke came ashore and loped toward her.

"You can drive the mules, but I'm going to walk along with you until I calm down," she said. When the boy refused to meet her eyes, she added, "You see, this is the first time I didn't stay in the cabin when we went through the tunnel."

Now Zeke looked straight at her, and Kate had to struggle not to laugh at his shocked expression. "I knew it wasn't right to expect somebody else to do something I was scared to do, so I made myself take the mules through when you—um, when you didn't want to. And you know what? It wasn't any worse than when I hid in the cabin. Not much worse, anyway, and it didn't seem to take nearly as long. I'll walk along with you next time," she offered. It would be easier next time, she told herself, and easier still every time she did it.

But Zeke shook his head emphatically and tapped his chest.

"Well, let me know if you change your mind. We'll have to make sure to use the other team, after the way Cupid and Junior acted today. I guess you heard them."

Zeke rolled his eyes, and Kate grinned ruefully and said, "I don't think I'll ever forget that sound." A chill ran down her spine.

From the boat, Seth called, "Tee, yip, YA-ah!" and Kate and Zeke stopped to wait for *The Mary Ann* to drift closer. "It's time to change teams," Seth called.

"He should have done that when he stopped before," Kate grumbled. She had bent to unhitch the team before she realized that not only was her stepbrother steering again, he was also making decisions that should be made by the captain. Kate straightened up, ready to protest, but then she shrugged and knelt to unsnap one of the chains on the harness. Seth had earned the right to steer again, and it didn't matter if they changed a bit late.

The boat nudged into the bank, and Seth wrestled the long mule fall board in place and urged General onto it. Seth *did* do a good job with the mules, Kate thought as Sandy followed his teammate to the ground, and he even seemed to like them now. She watched Cupid and Junior walk up the board and disappear into the stable, obeying Seth as easily as they did her.

What was it he said that first day? Something about how once he'd been to Georgetown and back, he'd know all about boating. Well, he was wrong. He was a good boater, but he certainly didn't "know all about boating," and it would be a long time before he did. He hadn't even begun to memorize the canal so he'd know ahead of time when they were nearing a lock, so he'd know when a straight stretch was coming up, or a narrow place where it would be hard to pass another boat.

It would take Seth a lot of trips to learn all that, Kate thought as she helped Zeke harness the new team. But it shouldn't take him any time at all to learn the levels. Silently, she began to recite the litany Papa had taught her: First the nine-mile level outside of Cumberland, and then the three locks. Then the Narrows—that's a one-mile level, and after that . . .

Chapter Twenty-Seven

Rain fell in torrents, and the cabin shutters banged in the wind. Kate lay in the darkness, wide awake and reveling in the wild energy of the storm but hoping it would be over before morning.

Gradually the darkness lifted, and through the rain-streaked window opposite her bed, Kate could see the wavering black lines that were tree branches whipping in the wind. So, it wasn't going to let up. Well, boaters had to work no matter— *What was that?*

Across the room, Seth echoed her silent question. "What's that flapping noise?" he asked, sitting up.

Flapping. What could be flapping in the wind? "The awning!" Kate was out of bed and pulling on her oilskin raincoat. She took Mama's oilskin from the peg and tossed it to Seth. "If we don't fasten that canvas down, the wind will tear it off and blow it into the water."

Kate opened the door and was hit with the full force

of the gale. She ducked her head and climbed the few stairs to the tiller deck, where she saw that two sides of the awning sheltering the cabin and the tiller had come loose and were whipping wildly in the wind.

As Kate made a grab for it, the awning billowed upward, pulling loose from another support, and then the wind dropped. The canvas collapsed, nearly knocking Kate off her feet. As she struggled out from under it, she heard Seth ask, "Why don't we weight it down and put it back after the storm's over?"

"Because I don't want to steer without any shelter at all," Kate retorted. "Get Zeke up. It's going to take the three of us to do this."

"He's feeding the mules."

"Poor things, out in this weather all night."

Water dripped from the rim of Seth's rain hat and splashed on the front of his oilskin. "But you'll send us out in it all day without a second thought, won't you?" he challenged, glaring at Kate. "Haven't you ever heard the expression 'not enough sense to come in out of the rain'?"

Kate could feel the cold water running down the back of her neck, and she knew that even if they could get the canvas in place, it wouldn't help much in this wind. Remembering how miserable it had been to drive the mules in a storm, she asked, "Are you saying you think we ought to lay over?"

"We'd be crazy not to."

He'd said *we* instead of "you." And he wasn't even working the first shift. After he rubbed down the mules, Seth would be snug in the cabin while she steered and Zeke drove the team. Kate looked around to see a bedraggled Zeke coming toward them, wet hair and clothes plastered to his skin. "Bring the plank over here so we can use it to hold down the canvas," she called. "We're going to wait out the storm."

The expression of relief on Zeke's face made Kate wonder how she ever could have considered sending him out to drive the mules in weather like this. "Why didn't he get an oilskin?" she wondered aloud.

" 'Cause you didn't tell him to," Seth retorted, and Kate felt the burden of her responsibility for the older boy as she never had before.

Zeke returned with the plank, and Seth used his pocketknife to slash the cord that secured the awning to the left rear post. With the entire stern section free now, the three of them quickly spread the canvas flat on the cabin roof and held it in place with the plank.

A gust of wind blew rain into the cabin after them, and a shower of water flew from Kate's oilskin when she shrugged out of it. "Zeke, go get your other clothes so you can change. We'll rig up a blanket to give you some privacy." She added corncobs and more coal to the embers of last night's fire, then measured out oats and water to start the oatmeal for their breakfast. "You'll have to stir this while Zeke changes," she told Seth.

He draped one of his blankets over the rope he had strung across the front of the cabin, but he didn't reply. What was the matter with him? Hadn't he heard what she said? He'd heard, Kate decided when she saw the stubborn look on his face, and he didn't like it. "Do you mind stirring the oatmeal while Zeke changes?" she asked.

"I'll be glad to," Seth answered as Zeke burst into the cabin, followed by another gust of rain.

While Zeke changed behind the makeshift curtain, Kate straightened her rumpled blankets and pulled up the quilt, tucking it under her pillow. She couldn't remember the last time she'd made her bed. There was always so much to do—far too much for the three of them. How could she have imagined that she and Seth could manage by themselves?

"You can take over this pot," Seth said as he folded his blanket. "Zeke's dressed now."

Glancing at the older boy as she took her place at the stove, Kate saw that his wet hair was dripping onto his shirt collar. "Dry your hair, Zeke," she said, "and hang your wet things over that rope."

As Kate stirred the oatmeal, she watched Seth take the small rag rug from the center of the room and move it in front of the door to soak up the water they had tracked in. "I think we should clean the cabin after breakfast," she announced.

"I think we should play cribbage," Seth countered.

Kate's eyes turned toward the polished wooden board and the small box of playing pieces resting beside a deck of cards on the top shelf, right where Papa had left them.

"I can teach you to play," Seth said, heading for the shelf.

Kate was about to stop him when she heard an echo of Papa's voice saying, *You have to let go of me, Katie.* The words sent shock waves through her. What did he mean? When had he told her that? Suddenly she remembered how he had insisted on teaching her to swim even though Mama didn't approve. Closing her eyes so she could concentrate, Kate summoned up a picture of her younger self clinging fearfully to Papa while he treaded water. She could almost hear him saying, *I've taught you how, Katie, so let go of me now and show me that you can swim on your own.*

"Hey, are you all right? You're not going to faint again, are you?"

Kate's eyes flew open and she saw Seth looking at her anxiously, the game in his hands.

"I—I'm fine," she said, surprised to find that she felt lighter, the way she had when the water supported her once she finally did swim on her own. Surprised, too, that she didn't mind seeing Seth with Papa's game. "I already know how to play," she added, " 'cause I used to watch Papa and his friends."

She gave the oatmeal one last stir before she began to fill the bowls, frowning as she silently repeated Papa's words: You have to let go of me, Katie. . . .

As soon as breakfast was over, Kate and Seth began to play while Zeke watched. They were so engrossed in the game that they hardly noticed the storm, but Kate looked up when a shaft of pale sunlight spilled through the window.

"We can get under way now that the rain's stopped," she said. "Wear an oilskin, Zeke, 'cause water's going to be dripping off the trees for a while." She went outside, calling over her shoulder, "Come on out, Seth, and I'll help you put that canvas back."

Once the awning was in place again, they set off with Kate steering and Seth stationed in the bow to snag any floating branches with the pole he carried. Kate raised her face and breathed deeply, enjoying the cool freshness of the air. Just ahead of the boat, bramble bushes on the berm overhung the water, and she saw that each cane of every bush hung with droplets of water shining in the clear sunlight. "Like tiny pearls," she whispered.

Realizing that the first of the Oldtown locks was just ahead of them, Kate shouted, "HE-EY, LOCK!" If they were at Oldtown already, that meant they were only eighteen miles from Cumberland, eighteen miles from home and Mama. They'd be home tonight! "HE-EY, LOCK!" Kate called again. Where was that pokey lock tender?

Chapter Twenty-Eight

Kate could hardly contain her excitement as the skyline of the city came into view, silhouetted against the fading bronze of the evening sky. She turned to Zeke and said, "That's Cumberland—we're almost home. Look, there's the steeple of the Presbyterian church, and there's the hotel, all lit up like a house afire." She gestured to the pinpoints of light on the hillside and added happily, "Those are houses over there, and one of them's ours. I can hardly wait to see Mama again!"

At the tiller, Zeke shifted his weight, and Kate sensed his discomfort. "We'll leave *The Mary Ann* in the boat basin and walk back along the towpath and then up a long hill to my house," she said. "When we get there, you'll take care of the mules—they have a shed out back—and then one of us will come get you so you can meet Mama and Seth's little sister." Zeke frowned and shifted his weight again, and Kate said, "I'll tell them you don't talk. You don't have to worry—they'll like you anyway."

Zeke nodded and carefully steered the boat around a gentle curve. Kate watched the twinkling lights and hoped Mama wouldn't mind that they'd brought Zeke home with them, hoped Julia wouldn't be afraid of him.

The last mile seemed to take forever. And then *The Mary Ann* had to be tied up in the boat basin, and the sacks Zeke filled with coal when they were in Georgetown had to be loaded onto the mules.

Finally they were ready, and Kate led the way home, wearing her dress and bonnet. She tried to ignore the raucous noise that came from the saloons in the shanty town that had grown up near the basin. In just minutes, she'd see Mama again!

As they neared the house, Kate saw light streaming from one of the upstairs windows—her mother's room—but the rest of the house was dark. Julia was keeping Mama company, Kate thought, and her steps faltered.

"Go *on*," Seth said, nearly bumping into her. "What are you stopping for?"

Cupid nuzzled Kate's ear, and Kate absently rubbed the mule's neck as she looked up at the window. Ignoring Seth's question, she started for the house. "Take Zeke back to the mule shed and help him unload the coal," she said over her shoulder.

"Zeke can manage by himself," Seth said, thrusting his mules' leads at Zeke and hurrying after Kate. He was right behind her as she ran up the steps of the back stoop and burst through the door.

"Mama! Mama, we're back!" As Kate ran down the narrow hall to the stairs, she barely noticed Julia brush past her, calling her brother's name. Moments later, Kate was in her mother's bedroom. "Mama!" she cried, throwing herself into her mother's outstretched arms, "Oh, Mama, I missed you so much."

"And I missed you, Katie," Mama said, holding her close. "How I missed you! Poor Julia tried her best to cheer me up, but it was my Katie I wanted."

A wave of feeling flowed over Kate, and she began to weep. Mama patted her and made little comforting sounds until Kate drew a long, shuddering breath and pulled away.

"Here," Mama said, reaching for the handkerchief on her bedside table, "let me dry your tears and take off that bonnet so I can have a real look at my girl." And before Kate thought to stop her, Mama had untied the bonnet and lifted it off.

"Oh!" Mama cried, staring from the dangling braids to the tousled ringlets that covered Kate's head. "What on earth—"

Kate heard a snort of smothered laughter behind her and turned from her mother's shocked face to see a man seated in a chair, his bandaged leg propped on a footstool. "You!" she exclaimed, flustered and relieved at the same time.

The man nodded. "Yes, me. Home from the war and a little worse for wear."

"Papa!" Seth cried from the doorway. Kate watched him struggle for composure as he looked from the smiling face to the bandaged leg and then crossed the small room to kneel beside his father's chair. The man reached out and pulled Seth against his chest, and the boy threw an arm around his father's shoulder. His voice muffled, he said, "I'm glad you're home, Papa."

"So am I, son. So am I."

"It's been far too long since all of us were home together," Mama said, beckoning to Julia who stood hesitantly in the doorway. "Come in, dear."

Dear! Kate caught her breath. *Dear!* And then, in the sudden silence, she saw that everyone's eyes were on her.

Julia's wide with apprehension, Seth's wary, and his father's— As Kate looked into the man's eyes, she saw a challenge, and confused, she turned to her mother. Mama smiled, and her face seemed to glow with contentment.

Kate turned back to Julia, and now the fearful look on the younger girl's face embarrassed her. Remembering all her good resolves, she said, "You can sit here by me if you want to. There's room."

"Seth told me how brave you were," Julia said, perching tentatively at the foot of the bed.

Of all the things Seth could have said about her, he'd said that she was brave. Not hateful, not bossy, not headstrong or stubborn, but brave. Confused, Kate traced the pattern of stitches on the bedspread with her finger. "Seth was brave, too," she said at last, and looking up, she met her stepsister's eyes. "Julia, you should be proud of your brother. After just one trip, he's almost as good a boater as I am." There. She'd admitted it.

"We're all proud of you both," Seth's father said, "and we want to hear how the two of you managed to take that boat to Georgetown and back."

The two of them. "Zeke!" Kate cried as Seth ran out of the room and clattered down the steps. "We had some help," Kate said, and turning to Mama she explained. "Mrs. Connally's youngest son, Zeke, came with us as crew. Seth's getting him now."

Mama frowned and asked, "You mean that big, gangling boy who doesn't speak? And you've brought him home with you?"

Hearing the displeasure in her mother's voice, Kate said, "Zeke's a good person, Mama, and he works hard. Besides, he'll just be here one night, since we're leaving again tomorrow. Or maybe day after tomorrow," she amended when she saw her mother's frown. Then, hoping to forestall an argument, she fluffed her curls and asked, "How do you like my new hairstyle?"

"It's becoming to you," Mama said, "but I don't understand why you cut it—or why you did this." She held out the bonnet with the braids dangling from it.

"I knew you'd be embarrassed if anyone saw me driving the mules, so I cut my hair and dressed in Seth's extra clothes so folks would think I was a boy hired on as crew. I did *that*," she continued, gesturing toward the bonnet, "so I wouldn't look funny when I wanted to wear a dress. Mrs. Connally's the only one who knows, and she promised not to tell."

Lowering her voice when she heard footsteps on the stairs, Kate said, "Here they come. Just talk to Zeke like you would anybody else—he'll understand what you say."

Mama looked doubtful, but when Zeke came into the room, hands in his pockets and shoulders hunched with embarrassment, Seth's father said, "Well, Zeke, I want to thank you for helping out on *The Mary Ann*. I understand you're a hard worker."

Kate's mind reeled. Her stepfather had called the boat by name—and he knew how to talk to Zeke! For a moment Kate had the feeling she was seeing the man for the first time, but then he seemed very familiar—an older version of Seth, with the same decency, the same ability to size up a situation and do whatever was called for. Not wanting to be caught staring, Kate turned to Zeke and saw the boy's face break into a slow smile even as he looked down at the floor.

In a strained voice Mama said, "I'm sure Zeke must be tired, Seth. Why don't you take some blankets out to the—"

"He can stay in my room," Seth said cheerfully. "It's small, but not as small as the hay house." The boys left the room, and Seth called over his shoulder, "Don't tell them anything about our trip till I'm back, Kate."

She wouldn't even know where to start, Kate thought, hoping Seth wouldn't be gone long. She stole a look at her stepfather, then quickly lowered her eyes again when she found him studying her. Still feeling his gaze, Kate's anger began to rise and she locked eyes with him, determined to stare him down. But to her surprise, he smiled and said, "Your mother's right about that haircut. It's becoming to you."

Seth's return saved Kate from replying, and the next hour was filled with excited talk. At last Mama said, "A break in the canal wall, a thief trying to rob you—and all that time I was worried about how you were managing the locks and whether you were keeping warm and dry." She leaned back on her pillow, and Kate saw her hand move to rest on the swell of her stomach.

"Are you all right, Mama?" Kate asked, but her mother wasn't listening. She was watching Seth whisper something to his father, who nodded and reached for the crutch beside his chair.

"Will you ladies excuse us for a moment?" he asked, struggling to his feet.

After he and Seth left the room, Kate asked again, "Mama, are you all right?"

"I'm fine, Katie," she said, smiling. "Now don't you worry, because by the end of the summer I'll be my old self again. And I'll have a wonderful surprise for you, too."

A wonderful surprise, indeed. It wouldn't be a surprise, and it wouldn't be wonderful, but it might be—interesting. "We know about the baby, Mama," Kate said impulsively.

Mama's eyes widened. "But how—"

"I heard you tell Mrs. Steller."

Mama frowned, but at the thump of a crutch in the

hallway outside the door, she let the subject drop. "Shh, here come our menfolk," she warned.

Kate watched Seth's father carefully lower himself into his chair, perspiration beading on his forehead with the effort. When he finally lifted his leg to the footstool, he leaned back and closed his eyes for a moment, and Kate wondered how she could have hated him so much. But when he opened his eyes again, his words put her on guard.

"Seth tells me that you want to continue to carry coal from Cumberland to Georgetown for the rest of the boating season, Kate," he said.

Nodding, she said, "We need the money, sir."

"Now that I've collected some of my back pay, renting out the boat and the mule teams would bring in all the money we need. What's wrong with that idea?"

"Everything!" Kate burst out. "Renters would mistreat our mules, and they wouldn't take good care of the boat, and besides, we're a boating family. Boating is what we do!" Papa would want us to stay on the canal, she added silently.

Mama said, "You know we can't allow you children to go down the waterway alone, Katie. You wouldn't have sneaked off the way you did if you didn't understand that. It's simply out of the question. You'll have to send that boy Zeke back home tomorrow with some other family that's headed for Georgetown."

Kate stared at the floor and didn't answer. They *had* sneaked off, and it *was* out of the question for them to go down the waterway again now that Mama had forbidden it. Kate would have been almost glad for an excuse not to make the difficult trip again if it hadn't been for the mules. The poor, poor mules! And poor Zeke. What if—

"Tell her what you decided, Papa," Seth urged.

"Your mother's right, Kate," the man said quietly. "We can't allow you children to go down the canal alone."

Kate swallowed hard and willed herself not to cry.

"However," Seth's father went on, "in another week or so, I should have recovered enough to go with you."

When Kate looked up, Seth was beaming across the room at her, but all she could manage was a trembly, "Go with us?"

"Not to be captain," Seth quickly explained. "Just to be the adult."

Kate's mind raced. Maybe with an adult along, boating would be a pleasure again instead of seeming such a burden. Since she was the one with experience, she'd still be in charge of the boat and the mules, but she wouldn't have to be responsible for everything else. Responsible for Zeke. "We could use an adult on our crew," Kate said. "Thanks."

For the second time that day, she felt lighter, but this time it was as though she had put down a heavy load, one much too heavy for a person her size. For a person her *age*. Suddenly she was aware that Julia was speaking.

"Can I come along, too?" she pleaded. "I'm not brave like Kate, but I'll do my best."

" 'May I,' not 'can I,' " Mama corrected automatically. "And yes, you may, if your father agrees—and if Mrs. Steller will stay here with me while you're gone. You deserve an outing after waiting on me all this time."

"Would you mind terribly if I came along, Kate?" Julia asked shyly.

Kate shook her head. "You can keep the cabin tidy and do the cooking. I'll show you how to make bean soup."

"Then that's settled," Mama said. "And next year, all of us will go."

"Even the baby?" Julia asked.

"She said 'all of us,' didn't she?" Kate said, reminded of

the boating family that had passed in the dusk on their first day out of Georgetown. "We can take turns helping with the baby, but since I'm older, my turns will be longer."

Seth asked, "But Katie, who will be the captain while you're being the mother?"

His question was greeted with laughter, and Kate felt the blood drain from her face. How dare they laugh at her! And then beside her, Julia whispered, "Seth's teasing, Kate—that's what brothers do. Please don't be mad."

What brothers do. And he'd called her "Katie." Thinking again of the boating family she'd envied so, Kate said, "Well, maybe by next year your father can be the captain, Seth."

"You—you'd let my father be captain of *The Mary Ann*?"

"Being the captain isn't as much fun as I thought it would be," Kate admitted. "It's not nearly as much fun as being the captain's daughter." Her heart sank when she saw tears of joy on Mama's face. That wasn't what she'd meant at all! Didn't Mama know she'd never be any man's daughter except her own dear papa's?

Her thoughts in a turmoil, Kate remembered that she'd promised Papa she would change, promised that she'd do better. She had made promises to herself, too—that she'd be a better daughter, that she'd try to please Mama. And now Mama was pleased, but—

Kate stole a glance at her stepfather. Flustered when she saw that he was watching her, she said the first thing that came into her mind. "What about Zeke? Can he still work for us when you come along to be the adult?"

"Of course. Seth can't drive the mules the whole day."

"All three of us will drive the mules, sir, just like we did this trip," Kate said, hoping the "sir" kept her from sounding defiant.

Mama frowned, but before she could object, her husband said, "I think that's reasonable, Kate, but from now on, you'll wear your own clothes. In wartime, women and girls often do work that's usually done by men and boys."

She was actually having a conversation with her stepfather, Kate marveled. He was listening to her as though he was interested in what she had to say, and he seemed to understand how she felt about boating. "Can I—that is, *may* I call you 'Captain' starting now?" Kate asked hesitantly.

"Captain it will be. And I'll call you 'my right-hand girl,' if that's all right with you."

Kate was glad he knew enough not to try to call her his daughter. "I'd like that," she said.

Mama squeezed Kate's hand and whispered, "I'm so glad to have my Katie back home."

Kate meant to say, 'It's good to be home again,' but she heard herself say, "It's good to be Katie again." She felt her face grow warm, but to her surprise no one laughed. And then she realized that what she'd said was true—it *was* good to be Katie again.

THE C & O CANAL

Today, the C & O Canal and its towpath are used for year-round recreation. The pastoral setting attracts bird-watchers and other nature lovers as well as the walkers, joggers, cyclists, and cross-country skiers who enjoy the towpath's smooth surface. Those who are looking for a tranquil place to fish, canoe, or ice-skate are drawn to parts of the waterway that have been restored.

But at the time of this story, the C & O Canal was a busy workplace. From early spring until the water froze the next winter, long wooden boats carried coal or grain and other products down the 184.5-mile-long waterway from Cumberland, Maryland, to Georgetown, in Washington, D.C. The boats were pulled by mules that walked along the towpath beside the canal.

The boat's crew, often a family, lived in a tiny cabin at the stern (back) of the boat during the trip, and an extra mule team was stabled at the bow (front). Corn and hay for the mules were stored in the "hay house" in the middle.

Canal boating wasn't particularly hard work. A woman whose family boated early in the twentieth century told an interviewer, "I have seen a ten-year-old girl take a boat through a lock." The work could be tedious, though, with six-hour shifts at the tiller, steering the boat, and six-hour shifts of walking beside the mule team. And someone had to care for the mules and do the cooking and housekeeping chores, as well.

Most crews had between three and five people, depending on whether they stopped for the night or kept going around the clock, but occasionally just two men would run a boat. At one time, a pair of brothers, one about fourteen and the other twelve, crewed a boat during the months their father was ill.

"C & O" stands for "Chesapeake and Ohio," because the canal was supposed to link the Ohio River at Pittsburgh with the Chesapeake Bay by continuing down the Potomac River from Georgetown. (Above Georgetown, rapids and falls make the Potomac unnavigable, so the canal was built alongside the river to allow trade between East and West.)

But by the time the canal reached Cumberland, in western Maryland, building expenses and difficulties had been much greater than expected, and since railroads were beginning to carry freight, it didn't make sense to follow the original plan. Although the canal was built for only half the distance initially intended, its name was never changed.

The C & O Canal was busiest and most profitable during the 1870s, though it continued to operate until it was badly damaged by a flood in 1924. After that, it was abandoned. The towpath eroded, and trees began to grow in the empty waterway. At one time, there was a plan to turn the route of the canal into a scenic highway, but officials gave up that idea after a group of hikers (including Supreme Court Justice William O. Douglas) publicized the area's natural beauty.

Today, the route of the C & O is protected as the Chesapeake and Ohio Canal National Historic Park. Although not all of the canal itself has been restored and rewatered, the entire towpath is maintained. Park visitors can see the locks and aqueducts that boaters like Kate and Seth passed through on their way from Cumberland to Georgetown—and they can walk through the tunnel that filled Kate with such fear.